BLOODY VIKINGS

UNKNOWN TRUE LIES
FROM THE NORWEGIAN SAGA

Bloody Vikings

Unknown true lies from the Norwegian Saga

by

Tore Fauske

Illustrated by Arne Gytre

The Pentland Press Limited
Edinburgh · Cambridge · Durham · USA

© Tore Fauske 2000

First published in 2000 by
The Pentland Press Ltd.
1 Hutton Close
South Church
Bishop Auckland
Durham

All rights reserved.
Unauthorised duplication
contravenes existing laws.

British Library Cataloguing in Publication Data.
A catalogue record for this book is available
from the British Library.

ISBN 1 85821 762 8

Typeset by George Wishart & Associates, Whitley Bay.
Printed and bound by Antony Rowe Ltd., Chippenham.

This book is dedicated to all who buy it. Bless you all!

START HERE:

This book is aimed mainly at visitors who would like to know something about Norway and the country's history. Although, 'visitors' is hardly the correct word here: 'anyone not educated in Norway, and therefore not familiar with the country's history, and who would like to know something about it', might be a far better description. Perhaps with: 'and who can read and understand, but not necessarily speak, English', just to make it absolutely clear.

This is, to express it in modern marketing language, the target group.

The book is devised in such a clever way that you can learn about our history in one of two ways:

1: You may be satisfied with just the bare facts; no frills, no detailed descriptions, no nonsense, nothing but the bare facts. If so, the index pages will probably suffice, and you may then give the book to a friend or relative.

2: You may want to know a bit more than the bare facts, i.e. the background, what happened next, how it all came about, and why, and who did what. In short, you want some meat on the bones.

If you belong to the first group, the index pages will, as stated, give you enough basic knowledge to be able to prove that you really know Norwegian history next time you are surrounded by natives of that country, be it at a dinner party, a meeting, on an aeroplane – wherever, by casually saying something like: 'Oh yes, wasn't that about 6 years before Olav Trygvasson was killed onboard that splendid ship *Ormen Lange* near Svolder?' or 'Did you say your name is Harald? That's a famous enough name in Norwegian history, knocking out 31 opponents down there in Hafrsfjord, thus uniting the whole country into one'. (Don't worry if you can't pronounce 'Hafrsfjord' properly, a lot of Norwegians even have difficulties here, especially if they have loose teeth.) – then quickly change the subject before anyone has a chance to express their delight and surprise at your familiarity with Norwegian history and leads you headlong into a discussion about the finer, and to you, totally unknown points as to HOW the same O.T. came to meet such a sad end or WHY and HOW Harald went into that battle. That is assuming at least one in your audience can speak English. But since most Norwegians do, and the ones who don't think they can, and often do after a couple of drinks, this shouldn't be a problem. And *if* your bluff should be called by some persistent Norwegian with an intensely burning interest in Norway's history in general and the Vikings in particular, leaving you fumbling and at a complete loss to understand what he's talking about, you still have an emergency exit available that should see you out of trouble: the language barrier. You simply say that you misunderstood him; not, of course, you hasten to add, because he does not speak good English – goodness, he does! – but because he seems to speak it with a rather strange Norwegian accent which you have never come across before. 'And by the way,' you say, (and if this lifeline does not get you out of trouble, once and for all, you have in all probability had it) 'talking about accents and dialects, do you have the same problem with dialects in Norway that we have in my country? Some are quite difficult to understand, even for a native of that country.'

That SHOULD do it. It will surely be a bad host who, after such a clever manoeuvre, will want to revert to the original subject. If he does, the only advice available is: Don't accept next time you are invited to his party. That shouldn't be a problem either since you probably won't be.

If you belong to the second group, that is if you want go beyond the index pages and read the whole book, you will be in a very strong position and have a great advantage over virtually *any* Norwegian you might meet, bar the odd Professor of Norwegian History or two, since you will know more about the country's Viking times than the vast majority of Norwegians, simply because of the Law of Inevitability, which you will not be subject to, and which states, quite briefly, that any subject rammed down your throat at school inevitably becomes extremely boring to the extent that you learn the minimum necessary for the exams, and you forget the maximum possible immediately following the exams.

And since Norwegians are no different from other educated people, nearly all of them have a vague recollection that someone called Harald, or Olav, or whatever, did something worth remembering, way back all those many years ago, without being able to pin-point it more accurately. Very, very few will be willing, let alone able, to contradict you when you show off with some of the details you will learn from this book.

As if that's not enough, the reading and digesting of this book gives you another and perhaps equally great advantage over at least 4.1 million of the population of about 4.2 million, giving you a flying start and easy race: whilst school books are dry, factual, lifeless, just names, figures, and years, you are now holding in your hands a book which brings history to life, gives you details and interesting snippets of information most Norwegians never had or even knew existed, at the same time – and this is worth noting: *at the same time as it gives you all the correct, relevant facts, dates, and places.* WHAT MORE DO YOU WANT?

Not much, we should think.

AND CARRY ON HERE:

If you have read anything about Norwegian history at all, you may perhaps discover that some of the names of the Norwegian kings, translated into English, do not necessarily correspond to the names you may have learned already. Don't despair – it does not mean you are confused or remember wrongly. All it means is that this book gives a fresh look at the Viking period, and as such, it has been decided to give a straight and literal translation of all names and nicknames. 'Olav den Hellige' is a good example: his name has many times been translated into English as 'St Olav', but we feel this is not strictly correct – neither he nor anyone else could be a SAINT whilst still inhabiting this Earth, doing battle all over the place. So in this book his nickname has been translated literally as 'Olav the Holy'.

Just as a matter of clarification.

INDEX

The Bare Facts:

Norway is united into one single kingdom under King Harald Hårfagre (865-933) (Harald the fair-haired) in 872 (The Battle in Hafrsfjord, Stavanger.)   38

Håkon den Gode (945-960) (Håkon the Good) brought up in England, brings the first taste of Christianity to Norway (Killed in battle near Bergen, about 960, which was both most unfortunate and very clever since Bergen had not yet been founded.)   47

Olav Trygvasson (995-1000) brings even more Christianity to Norway (before being killed in the battle near Svolder, Germany, on the first Millennium: year 1000, easy to remember.)   54

Olav Haraldson (1015-1030) (Olav the Holy) christened all the rest of the country (much against the wish of many, but still. Killed during the battle at Stiklestad, near Trondheim, in 1030)   58

Harald Hårdråde (1047-1066) (Harald the Hard Ruler) (nothing much Christian about him, waging constant wars against Denmark, and taking on England at Stamford Bridge in 1066, thus diverting the English forces away from the Channel Coast and William the Conqueror (who probably wouldn't have conquered much had it not been for HH). HH was killed at Stamford Bridge – 'serves him right!' according to some sources.)   64

Olav Kyrre (1066-1093) (son of Harald Hårdråde) and the exact opposite of his father, 'Kyrre' meaning 'the peaceful one'. (He was so peaceful that he founded Bergen, Norway's second largest city, in 1070, and it is hard to find a more peaceful place outside the football season.)   69

Magnus Barfot (1093-1103) (Magnus the bare-foot). (The last Viking to sit on the Norwegian throne. His only claim to fame seems to be that he always wandered around with bare feet. He was killed in Ireland whilst looking for food for his men.)   71

Sigurd and Øystein Magnusson (should, perhaps, not really be here, but being the sons of Magnus the Bare-foot, they round the whole thing off.)   71

You may well have noticed (i.e. you *should* have noticed) that there are the odd gaps in between the kings here and there: OLAV TRYGVASSON died in the year 1000, for example, but the next king given here, OLAV THE HOLY, does not appear until the year 1015. That does not mean that Norway was without leadership and a firm hand, drifting happily along, during those 15 intervening years. Far from it. Every so often, some *jarl* (earl) or *høvding* (chieftain) would pop up and exercise some sort of rule for a while, either alone or jointly with some like-minded earls or chieftains from other parts of the country. In musical terms these were mere interludes, and it would complicate matters enormously to include them here. Remember: THIS IS NOT A TEXT BOOK FOR USE IN SCHOOLS!

(After Olav Kyrre we even had what every proper nation seems to have sooner or later: a Civil War. But true to our national characteristics, of which common sense is one of the most pronounced, we soon realised the utter stupidity and futility of a civil war – a total waste of time and effort both of which could be spent in a much better and wiser way by fighting the Swedes and the Danes. So it didn't last all that long. But at least we have *had* one.)

Finally, in case you are uncertain about the correct pronunciation of some names: The

Norwegian alphabet has 29 letters, the last three – or 'additional ones', to you – are æ (Æ), ø (Ø), and å (Å), in that order.

The 'æ' is pronounced more or less as the 'a' in 'carrier' (at least that will do); the 'ø' as the hesitant 'Eh . . . ' as in 'Eh – I don't know', whilst the last one, the 'å', is easy: as the 'a' in 'saw'.

The trickiest one is the letter 'y'. There is no equivalent sound in English – the best thing you can do is to ask a Norwegian – any Norwegian – to demonstrate it. Even then . . .

Now read on, and you will be able to hold your own, historically speaking, amongst most Norwegians; probably all the Danes, and most definitely amongst all the Swedes.

If you belong to Group 1, we'll wave goodbye to you at this stage, whilst those belonging to Group 2, or who may have been given this book as a gift by someone in Group 1, will eagerly turn to the next page and read on, learn a lot, and close the book after the last page, wiser and more knowledgeable than Group 1 has ever been.

FOREWORD

WHERE OR WHEN DOES NORWAY'S HISTORY START?

This is a difficult question, and to find the right answer is even more difficult. There are those who think one should go all the way back to the period when all of our country was covered by a thick layer of ice and snow; the period described by the somewhat older inhabitants as, 'The days when we really *had* winters!'. But others maintain equally firmly that it is neither necessary, nor desirable, to go back as far as that, since talking about a country's history before it has any inhabitants is nothing but the purest nonsense. This latter category of historians therefore waits until the snow has melted and the ice has virtually disappeared, only remaining on some mountain-peaks, reaching down into some high valleys where they are called glaciers and are much admired by tourists – before they started counting historic years. In other words: roughly at the time when a tribe belonging to Homo Sapiens somehow strayed, probably unwittingly and possibly also unwillingly, way up north, thus laying the very foundation for our proud history. These, the first Norwegians, survived by hunting, moving about with the seasons and the animals they hunted – each and every one of them a mixture of a tough Tarzan and a nimble Mohican.

Although – it is hardly quite correct to call this tribe 'Norwegians' – don't forget that Norway did not exist at all at that time, it was totally and utterly unknown. It was not even a white area on the map – indeed, there was not even a map it *could* be a white area on. It will therefore seem extremely unlikely that this tribe, dressed in animal skins, and for some strange reason or the other dragging their women-folk behind them by the hair, would have nodded in recognition and said to themselves as they spotted another fur-clad human, also dragging a woman behind him: 'I say, there's another Norwegian!'

They might just as well have called themselves 'Swedes'. '*Kjølen*' (The Keel – an area full of bogs and heights forming part of the border between Norway and Sweden) was undoubtedly in the same place in those days as it is today, but would these people in any way have realised the significance of it? Hardly.

It is therefore clear that it is not correct to talk about Norway's history at this early stage of the country's development. We have to wait a few years.

'But,' an impatient soul may now ask, 'when DOES Norway's history begin? At which incident or at which year can we draw a strong, firm, Norwegian line and say categorically that THIS is where our country's history starts?' You may well ask. Where on earth *does* it begin?

> *This is the right place to mention an incident which may well be unknown to most: a beautiful summer's day in 1995, a farmer in the southern part of Norway, Klaus Nilsen Nyberg (he has a farm at Vanse, near Farsund), discovered an unusual mark in the soil when he used a lever to move a large boulder right on the edge of a field. Nyberg, who was completely self-educated, realised immediately the enormous significance of this mark, and a closer examination made it clear that he really had made an extremely rare discovery: this was where Norway's history started!*
>
> *However, a carbon analysis of the mark showed that the find is from the tertiary period, i.e. well BEFORE prehistoric times, so Nyberg's conclusions are based on wrong assumptions. But this has in no way prevented the formation of a Historic Society, said to have several members and which regards the place as a shrine to which all Norwegians have to make a pilgrimage at least four times during their lifetime.*
>
> *Nyberg is a reasonable chap, charging a mere NOK 5.- per person.*

Klaus Nilsen Nyberg points to the spot where, in his opinion, Norway's history started.

The fact that Nyberg has marked the spot with a Norwegian flag does not, quite frankly, make his version more plausible: it is a well known fact that the Norwegian flag is of a much younger age!

Over the years, many a wise man and woman has tried to find the exact answer to this vexed question, but has had to give up and come to some sort of compromise: they have called the period before people learnt to read and write 'pre-historic', and the period AFTER this 'historic'.

Which means that a country's history starts the very moment the inhabitants learn to read and write.

But this theory does not hold water. Is it sufficient that, say, 10% of the population is able to read and write? Is that the moment when the country's history starts? Or do you have to wait until, say, 50% of the population can do so? Or 100% perhaps? If the latter, the world is this very day full of countries with no history whatever. Quite clearly a very unsound foundation for determining *when* the history begins.

Those not in agreement with the above theory – and there are many – maintain that the very moment you can start counting historical years for any country is the very moment the nomads stop nomading about and settle down to cultivate the soil and become farmers. But this is an equally wobbly foundation since it precludes a number of countries, such as Arabia, with its nomadic tribes moving about in the desert, to take just one example, from having any history at all. And what about North America, where the Indians moved about, following the animals they hunted, for hundreds and hundreds of years? Not only do the American Indians have a long history – they even have their own films! Hundreds – not to say thousands – of them! Which shoots an arrow clean through this theory as well. It holds no more water than any of the former theories.

From all this it should be evident that it is impossible to answer this question in a sensible, responsible, and fully satisfactory way. And since the purpose of this book is in no way to set itself up as Judge and Executor, but merely to retell the facts, the questions remain open. It will be up to later generations to give an adequate answer.

We shall instead give the answer to a question which has not yet been asked: this book starts with the Viking period. But this only poses another intriguing question: WHERE or WHEN does the Viking period commence?

Another open question which later generations will have to answer, but which may here be answered as follows: This book starts with Harald Hårfagre. Saying that, we are fully aware that voices will be raised in protest, asking why H.H. has been picked as the starting line? And that's why it REALLY starts with Halfdan Svarte (Halfdan the Black). But only just.

FOREWORD FINISHED

THE TEXT, AS SUCH, STARTS ON THE NEXT PAGE

NEXT PAGE

Text and indisputable facts: Tore Fauske
Illustrations and even more indisputable facts: Arne Gytre

THE VIKING PERIOD

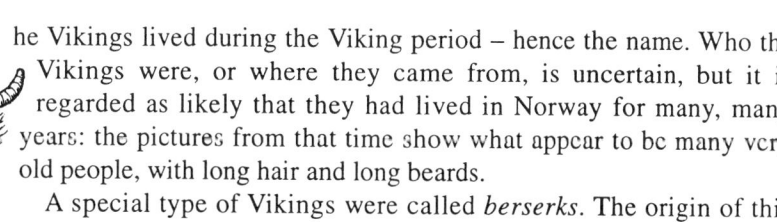

The Vikings lived during the Viking period – hence the name. Who the Vikings were, or where they came from, is uncertain, but it is regarded as likely that they had lived in Norway for many, many years: the pictures from that time show what appear to be many very old people, with long hair and long beards.

A special type of Vikings were called *berserks*. The origin of this name is not known for certain, but it has been assumed it comes from the term 'to run berserk', i.e. behave in an utterly wild and fearless manner, beyond any control or reason. (Note that this was a long time before football was even thought of.) The *berserks* were clad in bearskin, and many historians think that the name refers to this fact: '*bjørneserk*', literally 'bear shift', as in 'dress'.*

However, on second thoughts: is it likely that these fearsome and fearless warriors willingly and gladly would have accepted a name which, at least for one half of it, referred to a woman's garment? Hardly. So this theory should be forgotten, the quicker the better, – and should preferably not have been mentioned at all.

---

*This theory is quite interesting, because it shows that the Vikings were years ahead of their time, or, said another way: 'there's nothing new under the sun'. If the above is correct, it means that the *first* half of the Norwegian word 'ber' is a direct import and use of the English 'bear' (same pronuncation), whilst the *second* half 'serk' is as Norwegian as it can be. Compare this to today's Norwegian word for 'supply vessel, as used in connection with oil platforms: 'supplyskip'. Same pattern.

> *The berserks were undoubtedly the roughest and most terrible people ever seen in our country. In order to get some clothes on their body they not only caught bears, but in one single movement of one hand they simply ripped the fur complete, off the bear, leaving the poor animal without as much as one hair on its body. The unavoidable result was that the entire bear population in Norway was killed off by the severe winters.*
>
> *In contrast, the berserks paraded about in the warm and cosy bearskin without sending as much as a glancing thought in the direction of the bears. HOW BRUTAL CAN YOU GET?*

A naked bear is left without a hair on his body, shaking from cold, whilst the berserk has taken over all his fur.

Whatever the origin of the name the *berserks* were feared and fearless warriors. Indeed, they simply *loved* fighting, battles, war and unrest. During battles at sea they were always, without fail, standing right up in front at the sharp end of the sleek Viking vessels, using their bows and arrows, or swinging their axes and swords with such ferocity and strength that they cleared away anybody and anything which happened to be in their way. And in the middle of all this they shouted and yelled and screamed and carried on so loudly that they could be heard many miles away; at times all the way to VINLAND (now called 'USA'), where the natives thought this such a splendid idea that they immediately and without hesitation adopted the habit and made it their own.

Such shouting and hooting and yelling when attacking has forever after been called 'Indian's yell', and is a good example of how clever and skilful the Americans are when it comes to advertising.

Heads rolled in great numbers wherever the *berserks* fought, which was so often that it nearly bordered on always, and it did, quite frankly, seem to matter very little indeed whether these heads belonged to friends or foes, as far as the *berserks* were concerned. (Friends and foes did, naturally, look at it in a more subjective and different way).

The headhunters followed closely behind the berserks. In order to carry out this rather special work, they were mostly stubby men, preferably with a stoop, so that they could easily and efficiently bend down and pick up the loose heads.

This picture shows typical headhunters from Gvarv, Telemark, rolling heads into large piles for export to New Guinea, where there was a dearth of heads at that time. The natives on that island dried and shrank the heads and used them as amulets. (This is in all likelihood the very first, concrete example we have of Norwegian export in any form; clear evidence that the Vikings, far from being only fighters, robbers, burners, and sackers, were also interested in trade, both abroad and at home.) Today, such heads are priceless collectors' items.

Dried and shrunk Viking-head from New Guinea.

The *berserks* were, in other words, the H-bombs of their time, and were often quite handy to have around.

Unfortunately many did not feel kindly towards them and blamed them for the climate getting warmer, the glaciers melting, the harvest drying on the roots and the winters no longer being the winters they were in the good old days. We know now that these were unfounded allegations to the extreme, simply due to the fact that the Meteorological Institute and thus weather forecasting had not yet been established. Not that that would have made any noticeable difference; it's just worth mentioning.

Those studying history in more depth have long wondered why and how the *berserks* managed to work themselves up into such a frenzy that they were a danger to World Peace – at least to the immediate world surrounding them. It was not until new evidence was discovered partly by chance by two eminent Norwegian historians, and brought to public knowledge only within the last few years, that the answer to this puzzle was found: they were drug addicts. (Once more, the Vikings were ahead of their times.) This does not mean they sailed in *Vesterveg* (Viking-language for attacking the British Isles) with their superb vessels, loading them to the rim with opium, cocaine, morphine, and those sorts of thing, which they then smuggled ashore when they returned home. Not at all. If for no other reason: smuggling was an impossibility since the Norwegian Customs & Excise had not yet been invented.

No, they were far more skilful than to have to leave home on risky journeys to procure the necessary substances: they used home-grown produce – namely toadstools, normal, ordinary toadstools, growing to this day. They probably dried and ground the toadstools and mixed the powder with mead, and drank the concoction in large amounts and with great relish. Those who didn't die were used by the king as *berserks*.

And these *berserks* were in such great demand that the first any king did after he had managed

> *Little wonder that the berserks were feared by everybody, friends and foes alike. They were in many ways worse than their reputation. And that's no mean feat.*
>
> *Apart from all the terrible shouting, screaming, and yelling, biting the shields and chopping of heads, they had extraordinarily bad breath. And that's not strange: constant biting of hard, tough shields, making teeth shatter and splinter, with equally constant chewing of toadstools, or drinking of sweet mead full of crushed toadstools, is hardly the ideal recipe for mouth hygiene, and is strongly discouraged by dentists right up to this day.*

to kill all his opponents and a few non-opponents as well, just to be sure, was to criss-cross the country, looking for faithful *berserks* to serve him. Hence the term 'Go berserk', i.e. looking for *berserks*.

But let's be fair: not all the wars, conflicts, and non-peace could be blamed on the *berserks*. Anyone studying our history more carefully will soon realise that the main occupation of virtually every male – often eagerly supported and encouraged by the females – in those days, was to create unrest and fights. The vast majority regarded a day without fights, murder, and arson as totally wasted since you had to die in some form of battle to be let into Valhalla, the Residence of the Gods, whilst those who died from something resembling more natural causes, albeit they were probably few and far between, had to stand outside, looking in, wishing they hadn't.

An unsuspecting Viking suffers a severe stroke!

Perhaps that was just as well since it meant that large quantities of Vikings perished, one way or the other, every year. Had they not, some might well have survived to this day, creating severe problems for the UN, not to mention the enormous old-age pensions they would have been entitled to.

The Vikings did more, however, than just fight; they possessed many skills and – as already mentioned at least twice – in many ways they were up to hundreds of years ahead of their time.

Just take a skill like that of a shipwright. Here, the Vikings were supreme, designing, constructing AND handling their sleek, strong, fast sailing ships with what appears to have been effortless skills and dexterity, even crossing the Atlantic Ocean with them (see later). The North Sea they regarded as their own backyard, not to say local pond, such was their expertise in this field.

Both The UN and The Social Security Services may take it easy regarding the Vikings' life-span and possible negative consequences. Most of them were felled by a stroke. A fact which confirms our suspicion that their way of eating and living was not the healthiest-pork in every form and shape and plenty of beer and mead resulted in a population with a very high level of cholesterol in the blood. The result was only to be expected.

Those who did not die from a stroke (preferably against the head), either suffered another form of stroke – even heat-stroke (in very hot summers). No wonder the Vikings gradually became extinct.

We have found a number of these ships, well preserved. All have been found buried many metres in the ground, causing speculation that the sea-level has changed dramatically since the Viking times, since not even the Vikings would or could have used their ships *underground*.

> *It is quite correct that historians and archaeologists have wondered why not a single Viking ship has been found at or in the sea – only ashore. And normally many miles from the nearest lake or water. More recent studies would seem to indicate that the relevant Viking authorities refused point-blank to issue any Certificate of Seaworthiness for the vast majority of these ships, for the very good reason that most of them had been built purely with a view to dry-training (on land) of recruits to the Navy.*
>
> *So it is no more than a law of nature that these once so proud ships gradually sank down into, and disappeared in the often damp ground upon which they once stood. And that done, what was more natural for people living nearby than to throw old furniture and other household articles into the same hollow? And there you are: anyone then digging all this up, hundreds of years later, would inevitably come to the conclusion that when the owner died, the ship was buried with the owner and all the owner's possessions.*

Recruits from Queen Tyra's Household during a keen training session in a field near Oseberg. As one can see quite clearly, their handling of the oars leaves a lot to be desired, but after the compulsory 12 months National Service even the most die-hard landlubber from a mountain farm in the middle of the country could handle a Longship.

Although the ships we have found have not been launched again we have built exact replicas and they have all turned out to be highly seaworthy. Some have even been used in films, and Norway earns huge sums every year on the sale of miniature Viking ships. Without the Vikings this would not have been possible.

The Viking ships had to be rowed or sailed, for the sole reason that James Watt had, as yet, not invented the steam engine. So – once more a crystal clear example of the Vikings' foresight: they had the ship ready, and had had it ready for

Queen Tyra, fed up with the way the recruits handle the oars, gives a personal demonstration of how it should be done!

many, many years – it was not until hundreds of years later a foreigner got round to inventing something with which to propel the ships.

SO FAR, we have mainly dealt with the Vikings as warriors, peace-wreckers and general troublemakers, with some trade and other slightly more peaceful occupations thrown in here and there. This may possibly have given a slightly wrong and slanted picture, so this might be the right point to take a closer look at what could literally be described as the poetic side of their life. The *skald*.

A *skald* was, well, – we can do no better than to quote verbatim from Volume XV, Ser-Soosy, of The Oxford English Dictionary, Second Edition:

'skald, scald. *Usually applied to Norwegian and Icelandic poets of the Viking period and down to c 1250, but often without any clear idea as to their function and the character of their work'.*

As previously mentioned, and which everyone belonging to Group 2 will already have realised, this book gives you a lot for your money in the form of details and information you never knew existed and which you thought you could do without, thus living in blissful ignorance for many years.

As if this is not enough, we can now help out even the erudite editors/compilers of the above mentioned OED and tell them EXACTLY which functions the *skalds* had, and what their work was.

A *skald* was, as the OED quite correctly states, a poet. But that was only part of his job – and, it may well be argued, not even the main part. True, the *skald* was constantly putting quill to parchment, normally praising the king sky-high in a most flowery language – hardly surprising since the king was the one paying the *skald*, and even less surprising when you realise that a mere couple of wrong words, or words which could in any way be misinterpreted – and Swush! – one quick movement, and off came the *skald's* head. Just like that. So it paid amply to play safe.

A representative from the 'Literary Quality Control Board' (LQCB) makes sure that a famous, but unknown, skald, suddenly loses his head when reciting a poem obviously falling short of the quality requirements of the day.

> *Our far-seeing authorities introduced quality control for all literature already one thousand years ago.*
>
> *The penalties were hard, but then as now: artists had to be kept on a tight rein.*
>
> *The author seems to be slightly condescending when he writes that if the skalds used a wrong word – Swush! – off came the head.*
>
> *What he omits to say is that, if so, at least the head came off with the help of the long arm of the law!*
>
> *The quality control had been passed personally by the king, and ALL who could write knew exactly how far they could – or could not – go.*
>
> *That such a strict control over the written word has been a virtue of necessity also in more modern times, is clearly demonstrated by the examples set by such paternal figures as Benito Mussolini, Josef Stalin, Adolf Hitler, and Fransisco Franco, just to mention a few.*
>
> *If a majority of the skalds had not obeyed the legislation, the sources of this book would not have existed! Or vice-versa.*

But having said that, their main job (at least as seen from where we are today), was to *record* for posterity what was going on. Without the *skalds*, our knowledge of and insight into the Viking period would have been greatly smaller; virtually non-existent, in fact. Because they kept churning out poetry like there was no tomorrow (and, as we have seen, unless they were careful there wasn't), we have been given a pretty good picture of what went on, who did what, why, and where. This book owes them a great debt.

Anyone looking up the word '*Skald*' in a fairly decent Norwegian encyclopædia, will see that, on the whole, it agrees with the OED, but goes a little bit further by adding something like: '*The origin of the name is unknown*'. Again – and we say this without blushing – we are able to put things right, once and for all, hoping that later editions of these in other respects so excellent publications will see fit to amend their relevant entries about *skalds*. It is nothing but amazing that such statements as those quoted above have been able to survive, unopposed and unamended, for so many years, when the answer is obvious and has been staring everyone who cared to see straight in the face, all these hundreds of years:

The word *skald* comes from, and is closely related to, the word *skalle*. Or 'skull' in English. But add a 't' – skallet – and you get 'bald'. And the *skalds* had their hair cut to differentiate them from the real, fighting Vikings, to signify that they were different, slightly odd in a way, much as we regard poets today. And as a signal to the enemy in a battle – the moment a happy sword-swinger spotted a bald head in front of him, he knew he could spend his energy on better things than separating the bald head of a harmless *skald* from the rest of his body, whose only call in life was to string together lots of words, many of them preferably starting with the same letter or sound*, but was otherwise completely harmless. So they were basically left in peace to get on with their *laying* (poetry), often running from one battle to the other, reeling off words faster than you would think humanly possible, their bald heads shining like beacons if the sun was out. In addition, albeit without the reason for this being quite clear, their beards were also shaved off. Regularly.

*'Alliteration' is the technical term for this, and it was extensively used by the *skalds*. The first line from a famous lay (poem) demonstrates this technique in a clear, concise way: it is about Thor – the God of Thunder – waking one morning, discovering his famous hammer has disappeared, a very serious matter since without it, he is unable to produce thunder and lightning. The *skald* expresses it thus: *Vreid var Ving-Thor då han vaknadi*... (roughly: Wing-Thor was angry when he woke up ... [and who wouldn't be, if their hammer had been stolen during the night?[).

Once again, the Vikings showed that they were years and years ahead of their time: whilst an Englishman by name William Shakespeare has received great acclamation for his alliterative writings, it should not be forgotten that the Viking *skalds* showed him the way!

Due to the cutting method (read on), the hairdressing salons were called 'Blotir shops' – a name surviving to this day in the English 'Bucket shop', even if the meaning as such has changed. These 'Blotir shops' did not, of course, have the same standards as required today. The hair-cutting method was simple and very straightforward: a bucket was pushed down over the head of the customer – and you cut round it.

*There might well have been the odd drop of blood or two, and some ear-lobes probably disappeared as well, but what was that to a Viking? When a skald came in to have his hair cut, the same bucket was used, but now **without** its bottom.*

A satisfied customer is given a normal haircut.

*A **skald** is made ready for his weekly shaving and haircut. It can be seen very clearly that some found it difficult to relax. The patent with the bucket was so successful that it was seriously discussed as late as during the 1930s for use in all dental surgeries.*

So with a bald top, and no decorative beard – not even a moustache – it would have been truly extraordinary had these Viking-poets not been given the name *skald* – 'baldy', by their hairy and bearded contemporaries.

Today we have to be thankful and grateful to the *skalds*. Without their hard and often frantic work a huge slice of our proud history would have been totally unknown – not only to us, but also to the rest of the world. They were, as hinted already, the PR-people and news-reporters of their day, and – just like today – you have to take their statements with a pinch of salt. It was only natural that they exaggerated a bit here and there – the enemy's losses were, for example, always quoted as much larger than one's own – but nevertheless...

We will fail if we leave this particular subject without mentioning one particular *skald*, since it shows very clearly that for all their seemingly mild and meek manners and bald head and lack of beard, they did not lack courage and real Viking-spirit. We are, of course, alluding to Einar Tamberskjelve. 'Of course', since he must rank among the most famous of all Norwegians from that period – and his deeds and utterances are familiar stuff, held dear by any and everyone who has ever gone to school in Norway.

He was only 18 years when he was taking part in the Battle at Svolder (see *Olav Trygvasson*) in the year 1000. Perhaps unusually for a *skald*, Einar was an excellent archer, renowned for his strong bow and piercing arrows. He thought highly of his king, but considered him rather careless when it came to looking after – or not looking after – his bows and arrows. It would, of course, have been more than out of place for a *skald* – and a mere 17-18 year old *skald* at that – to criticise the king in any way, unless he had a strong desire never to reach his 19th birthday, but clever as he was, Einar hinted a couple of times in a very subtle way when reciting his latest lay to the king. So subtle, in fact, that no one noticed. Least of all the king.

Then came the Battle at Svolder. Since Olav Trygvasson was ambushed (see later) and had sent most of his ships ahead to find a suitable place to drop anchor, or possibly sack and rape – or both – since these ships were faster than his own and well-known very large *Ormen Lange*, every man present counted, which meant that Einar would have to forget all about alliteration, reporting, and running about chanting, and instead join battle, using his immense skill with his bow to defend his king.

And so he did with great success – until an enemy arrow hit his bow just as he was pulling an arrow back. It snapped with a crack so loud that King Olav heard it so clearly through all the shouting and yelling and general commotion, for all he did not stand anywhere near Einar, that he shouted: 'Whatever was that which cracked so loudly?'* Einar might be only 18, but no fool, and realising that without his bow and skills the battle was as good as over, with an unfortunate result as far as Olav was concerned, he shouted in an equally loud voice back to Olav: 'That crack, Sire, was the bloody country snapping out of your very hands!'

Olav, realising how serious the situation was, threw his own bow to Einar, saying he could borrow it until the battle was over. Einar took it, put an arrow on the string – and pulled the arrow a long way back, the point ending up far behind the bow. He thought the time had come to put it bluntly to Olav, threw him the bow back and said in the true manner of a *skald*: 'Too weak, too weak is the king's best bow. It serves the country badly to do battle with bent bows'. THEN Olav took the hint, but alas! it was much too late: he lost both the battle and his life, but there's every reason to believe that had he only listened to Einar earlier, the result would have been quite and happily different.

In those days the individual counted for little or nothing. What *did* count was the family. Family and relations were the all-important factors – blood was certainly much thicker than water, or even mead. It counted for everything. If a man was killed other than in battle (but even then it might depend on the circumstances), any member of his family was fully entitled to kill anyone belonging to the murderer's family – no matter how many times removed. Indeed, this was more than *entitlement*, it was a simple *duty*.

King Olav hears quite clearly a CRACK as Einar Tamberskjelve's bow breaks during the Battle at Svolder. We see quite clearly that the king's own bow is a mere toy in the hands of someone like Einar.

---

*As every schoolboy and schoolgirl in Norway knows: these are perhaps the most-quoted and most famous words in our entire history, and just like Winston Churchill's famous 'Never... have so many...,' they are constantly quoted, misquoted and used in all sorts of contexts. And rightly so. They were profound words.

It is not hard to imagine the complications and difficulties resulting from this custom. If, say, Olav Haraldsson was killed by Sture Geirson, it meant that *anyone* related to Olav Haraldsson could – indeed *should* – kill any member of the Geirson family he might happen to come across or stalk out.

The theory might well have been a sound one when first put into practice when all members of one and the same family lived perhaps on two or three farms only a furrow-length apart. But as families grew larger and people spread out to neighbouring hillsides and valleys, things got complicated and required some form of book-keeping: a member of the Haraldsson family might well meet a member of the Geirson family and kill him in revenge, thinking the slate was now clean, without knowing that the very same day another member of his family, in a valley on the other side of the mountain, also killed a member of the Geirson family. If then a THIRD member of the Haraldsson family killed someone from the Geirson family in HIS valley, things were on the point of getting out of hand: the Geirson family now being two down. But this would not be realised by either family until the next family reunion, when they would swap tales and count heads. In short: it gradually become impossible to keep track of who did what and where – and why. But it prevented a population explosion, and that it was an efficient, albeit not all that appealing, means, can be seen from the fact that the population hardly increased at all during the period.

It is worth noting that this, in our eyes, slightly unpleasant habit was taken up by the inhabitants of Sicily many years later, and given the name *Vendetta*. Curiously enough, this is an Italianisation of the Norwegian 'Hvem er detta?' ('Who is it?') which, as far as we know, were just about the only words the victims had time to utter as they were surprised by their murderer, normally in darkness.

But once more we might have led you to believe that the Vikings were nothing but bloodthirsty, yelling, fur-clad monsters. Nothing could be further from the truth.

They were in reality very friendly – and loved parties. During the winters they hauled their ships high up on dry land – they found no pleasure in bobbing up and down in stormy weather on a cold sea, never mind what riches were waiting on the other side, only to come home again to discover that the fjords were frozen solid. And lying there, by the edge of the ice, waiting for spring to come and the ice to go so they could get home at last, was something they found not all that appealing. So they stayed home and partied.

The Vikings called their parties *gilde*. And although all decent dictionaries translate *gilde* as 'party', it was much more than that. Should a Viking happen to be present at what we today call a 'party', he would raise his eyebrows in disbelief, thinking he had merely stumbled into a gathering of the most inexperienced party-organisers he had ever heard of. The Vikings partied for days – sometimes weeks – on end, without stopping. You may well ask what else could they do in the dark winter months but drink and party the whole season away, and you are partly right. But only partly.

The *gilde* was far, far more than just a party: it was an ingenious and infallible method of making sure you had no enemies. You simply invited all your enemies to a *gilde*, you all had a marvellous time, and at a certain stage in all the jollities, with everyone holding a horn full of mead in both hands, the host would excuse himself – saying he had to obey a call of nature, nip outside, lock the door – then he and his men would set fire to the house. Which meant you had no more enemies that winter. It also meant, of course, that you didn't have a house, but this seems to have been less important.

But this form of wild parties gradually died out, for two good reasons. Firstly, the insurance companies did not like it much, and when they became rather reluctant to indemnify against such events, stating that the excess would have to cover it all, people got equally reluctant to carry on this rather debatable habit.

Secondly, and perhaps equally important, was the fact that as the guests began to realise what was happening – or about to happen – they insisted on accompanying the host outside when he excused himself. And since it was rather pointless to burn down an empty house for which you would not get any insurance money, this somewhat unpleasant habit died out by itself. The direct result of the entire *gilde* – all obeying a call of nature at the same time, can be seen to this very day on some old and isolated farms where the 'three-seater' or even 'five-seater' outside privy is still in use.

It is a well-known fact that when Norwegians drink, we lift our glasses and say *Skål* (pronounced 'Skawl'). It has puzzled all serious historians for centuries why on earth we say '*Skål!*' (which in Norwegian also means 'Bowl') when we drink from glasses. It would be far more logical to say 'Glass!'.

It was not until recently that two eminent historians, partly by studying finds made by a young shepherd-girl in a remote valley in East Norway, and partly by reading and analysing what the *skalds* had to say, managed to crack what had so far been an uncrackable nut and reveal that this is probably one of the most ancient and well-established traditions in the world, having lasted unbroken for *at least* 1200 years, started by our hairy and bearded ancestors, and still going strong. And like so many vexed and seemingly unsolvable questions, once you have the answer, you wonder what all the difficulties were about. The answer has been staring us in the face all these years: alcohol in all its forms was very much cheaper in the Viking times than it is today, both in absolute and in relative terms, so the Vikings could well afford to drink directly from huge bowls filled with alcohol. There was quite simply no need whatsoever to go the long way round via small glasses.

Why you have to say anything at all when you are drinking also puzzled the historians for many years. But they have found the answer to this question as well: it was a dire necessity, literally a question of life and death. Since it was no longer fashionable or indeed possible to get rid of your enemies by roasting them alive when they were visiting you, the Vikings had to think out some other and equally effective way of solving this problem.

The answer was pretty obvious, really. Sit round the huge, wooden table, eat and drink well, and the moment your favourite enemy tilts his head back, concentrating on gulping down your mead in great quantities as fast as he can, thus baring his throat, you simply slit it, with one single, quick movement. And you have one enemy less – a fair amount of mess, true, but one enemy less.

This worked for a short time, but just like the habit of setting fire to the house, your enemies soon tagged on to what was happening, and in order to forestall any monkey business when their head was tilted temptingly backwards, they lifted their glass, looked you straight in the eyes and said '*Skål!*' (meaning 'Well, if I am going to drink, YOU are going to drink as well, so I can keep an eye on you!'). This increased the average life-span by 7½ years (disregarding all those who drank themselves to death).

After this general overview of the Viking period, we'll look more closely at some of the most important Viking kings. As already mentioned, we have chosen to start with Harald Hårfagre (Harald the Fair-Haired). That is, we have – and we haven't.

(This should really have been the end of this Chapter, but isn't. The reason is given on the following page).

FOLLOWING PAGE:

REASON:

There is a large minority, even, perhaps, a minor majority, who are adamant that the Viking period does NOT begin with Harald with all that fair Hair, but with his father, Halfdan Svarte*, so maybe it is only reasonable to give a very brief summary of his life, just to keep you right up to date.

Halfdan was king somewhere in East Norway (in this context it does not really matter exactly where), and he loved *gilder* and sledge-rides more than most, a lethal combination as it turned out, as far as he was concerned, since it became the direct reason for his demise. He had been to a great *gilde* which had lasted for many days and nights one late winter/very early spring, and was on his way back home, sitting comfortably wrapped in layers of fur and skin in the sledge, cheerfully pulled by two strong horses, no doubt looking forward to a last hornful of mead in front of a roaring fire before retiring to bed for the week.

His home was on the other side of a fjord called *Randsfjorden*, and when he had gone *to* the *gilde* all those many days before, the air had been full of minus degrees Centigrade, the snow crisp and the ice thick. Whilst he had been swinging the mead horns, singing songs and in general having a good time, the spring had approached quite rapidly, beginning to eat into the ice, making it generally unsafe.

So when the king and all his men arrived at the fjord's edge, he was implored by two local farmers who happened to be nearby to think twice before he ventured across. The king heeded

---

*The origin of this strange surname (literally: The Black One) is far from clear. Some historians believe he was the first coloured immigrant to Norway, a theory rejected by others as utterly preposterous, not least because his son had the fairest hair of them all, saying it is far more likely it was because he never washed properly. The king's Christian name – if one could have a Christian name in these wild days, well before Christianity made its entry into Norway – is, however, less of a puzzle, meaning 'Half Dane'. The only aspect of disagreement and discussion here is *which* half?

their advice – he thought twice, and *then* ventured across. Although, 'across' is not the most accurate word here, unfortunately: it was pretty dark, and the two farmers could not really see clearly what happened, but the next day, as daylight broke, they discovered a rather large, black hole only about 50 metres from the shore. It had not been there the day before, and since no one ever saw or heard any more of Halfdan, his horses or any of his men after that day, it seemed safe to assume that the whole jolly lot had gone through the ice. The best they could hope for was that they would be let into Valhalla, for all they had not died in battle. But there was still a chance, seeing Halfdan was a king.

And that's where Harald Hårfagre – he of the Fair Hair – comes into the picture: he was Halfdan's son.

THE (MOST IMPORTANT) VIKING KINGS

A: HARALD HÅRFAGRE (HARALD THE FAIR HAIRED)

Harald Hårfagre may well be regarded as Norway's Greatest King ever, and it is no exaggeration to say that Norway's history has him as its starting point. When he came to power at the tender age of 10 years (his father, Halfdan Svarte, drowned, remember?), Norway was far from a united country, but consisted of a large number of more or less independent areas, each one ruled by a local king or an earl. The country was, quite simply, full to the brim of local kings and earls; you could hardly move without bumping into them. Even the keenest student of Norway's history must shudder at the mere thought of having to try and sort out any lineage as to who was the son or daughter of whom, who ruled where and for how long. It would have been an impossible task, and if for no other reason than the one just mentioned, we should be ever thankful to Harald Hårfagre for not only deciding, but also managing, to push them all into total historical darkness, never to be seen or heard of again.

But there was a natural reason for this multiple division of the country. Norway has always been a very democratic society – indeed, our Constitution has been the model for a great number of other Constitutions around the world. It was therefore regarded as an obvious right at that time that since the country was not a republic, which might have given every inhabitant at least a theoretical chance of becoming President and Boss, well – the answer was to make every second citizen into a king or an earl, ruling a small area. Had Norway been one single and united kingdom, with ONE king only, this arrangement would quite clearly have been impossible, even if the odd slitting of throats and/or burning of houses might open the door for a handful of citizens now and then. The solution was obviously numerous small kingdoms with numerous little kings and earls.

But Harald did not think much of this arrangement. Not because he wanted power or wanted to rule all alone, far from it. He was probably not only our, but the world's first real statesman. It is no exaggeration to say that he foresaw the UN, EFTA, EU, and all – if ever there was a man hundreds and hundreds of years ahead of his time, with a crystal clear vision of Things to Come, realising that if we were to survive as independent nations we had to join forces, become bigger and stronger, be organised, it was indeed Harald Hårfagre. 'Organise and be strong!' he used to say, and he said it often. And nothing seemed more natural to him than that everyone should unite under his leadership. So he set out to unite Norway, and to prove it was not an empty promise, he swore he would not set his foot inside a *blotir shop* (hairdresser) until he had completely and permanently removed all these little kings, and earls, and chieftains, scattered liberally about on islands and mountain tops, in the valleys and forests and wherever else. He undoubtedly felt called to a Mission.

After thus having sworn not to have his hair cut until he succeeded, he started his campaign. He proved that statesmanship was not his only strength – he was also an eminent military tactician, working his way up strategically from the smallest and weakest earl, picking them off, one by one, like ripe fruit. As he progressed, his army grew since more and more people joined his ranks when they saw which way things were going, and in the end he had a huge fleet (there are those who say that Harald laid the keel for the Royal Norwegian Navy, whilst others say this is taking things a bit too far, the opinions are split), and several thousand men under his command. Everyone thought Norway had now been united into one single kingdom.

But in the south-west of the country, round Stavanger, there lived some farmers and kings and earls of a different opinion. They were scattered over a largish area from Stavanger and inland, away from the coast, over the flat area of Jæren, and decades full of strong winds, always blowing in the same direction, against them, and horizontal rain, had made them tough, wet, and stubborn, and they could see no reason whatever why they should have to disappear quietly out to the left and leave the scene to a chap with long, fair and probably curly hair – and from East Norway at that. So 31 of these local kings gathered somewhere in the Stavanger area and promised each other mutual support and aid and solidarity forever (in effect, some sort of miniature NATO) to repulse any attempt by HH to remove them. This agreement was sealed with a great *gilde*, so famous that our great playwright, Henrik Ibsen, even wrote a play about it many, many years later: *Gildet på Solhaug*. (The fact that Solhaug is nowhere near Stavanger, and the play doesn't really mention these 31 kings/chieftains at all, must be regarded as slight poetic licence on Ibsen's part.) That done, these 31 bold men returned home, took an aspirin, went to bed and waited for Harald.

They didn't have to wait long. Hardly had they rolled into bed before Harald's representatives knocked on their respective doors – a bit too hard, they thought – with a challenge to settle the matter once and for all. It was agreed that the fight should be over 32 rounds (one round for each of the 31 kings, and one for Harald), in a fjord – Hafrsfjord* – just outside Stavanger. It is true this would give Harald's opponents the advantage of home ground, but so sure was Harald of the outcome that he generously and readily agreed. It was furthermore agreed that the result would be binding on all parties. The winner would be proclaimed King of Norway for all Eternity. Which they all agreed was a long time.

Then D-day arrived. (Again, the Vikings were well ahead of their times). We know from the *skalds* that it was a most beautiful day with warm sunshine and a mirror-like fjord, and no wind. No wind, no rain, no clouds. There can be little doubt that this did influence the end result; indeed, it may well have been a deciding factor. The 31 kings and their local followers, all living on, in, or near the very flat Jæren area, were far from used to such weather – and it confused them, unbalanced them and made them uncertain: what had happened to the blustery winds from every direction and the pouring rain they had been born into, brought up in, and got used to? Who else,

---

*Next time you have guests, you may entertain them with a superb party game which will also show you which of your friends has or have a great sense of humour: give each participant three dry biscuits – such as crackers – and ask them to eat all three biscuits in one go, at the same time as saying 'Hafrsfjord' three times in quick succession. The result will normally, but not necessarily always, cause a certain amount of jollity. It is a fair bet that the one who leaves first and never invites you back, is completely devoid of any sense of humour.

being of a right and sound mind, other than someone from East Norway – used to this type of day with warm sunshine and no wind – would even consider battle on a day like this, instead of settling down in a cosy place in all this glorious sunshine, lying back and letting the rays from the sun soak warmly into a wet, or at least damp, body?

They felt like strangers, utterly lost in a most weird place, even before the battle had started. But there was no way back: time and place had been agreed, and an agreement was an agreement (the Vikings were gentlemen in this respect). Not only that: the combatants were lined up and ready, and the shoreline was already crowded with spectators – most of them having cast off their various types of fur, baring their sodden bodies to the warm sun. To postpone the battle was an impossibility.

Both parties had gathered all the ships and mustered all the men who in any way could carry and use any form of weapon. As was customary in those days, the bows of the ships were tied safely together, facing each other, making sure no one could escape. And right up front, as far forward as it was possible to get, nearly overhanging the bows like bowsprits, were the *berserks*, trembling with eagerness, impatience, and keenness, already yelling, banging their shields with their swords and biting them with their teeth, shouting the foulest insults to the opposition, spurred on by the encouragement from the spectators ashore. Every *berserk* had been given a double ration of toadstools that morning, and they were getting very near to being out of control. It was clear that if the battle did not commence pretty soon, it would be quite dangerous to be around.

So the start signal was given and the *berserks* let loose.

The *saga* tells us that never before had such a battle been fought on Norwegian soil. (Like Ibsen all those many years later, the *saga* obviously took some poetic licence, as the battle was not fought on any *soil* at all, but on *water*.) Literally facing each other was the very best of human resources Norway had to offer; the élite, the *crème de la crème* of fighting men – the most ferocious, wildest, strongest, and most fearless and fearsome *berserks*, the very best archers this side of the North Pole, the strongest sword swingers and the fastest talking *skalds* ever seen or

*The illustrator has here, albeit unwillingly, given a clear illustration of how misunderstanding and misreading a dictionary may so easily result in misillustration and mistranslation: the word used in Norwegian, as in the words surviving from the *skalds*, is 'flåte'. One of the meanings is 'raft', as used above and as illustrated. But the word also means 'fleet', as in 'a fleet of ships', which is obviously the meaning here. Harald would hardly take the time and trouble to chop down all those trees and build a huge RAFT, considering he already had a FLEET OF SHIPS at his disposal! And – if he did – what on earth was he going to do with such a raft once the battle was over? It would have been far too large to use for rafting – and, what is more: HARALD WAS SIMPLY NOT THE SORT OF CHAP TO DO SUCH A THING!

The most serious objection to the idea that the raft King Harald gathered (built) in Hafrsfjord was the very beginning of the Royal Norwegian Navy, is that it would be sheer madness to risk everything on one, single raft, virtually impossible to row.

A proper Navy requires a fleet of easily manoeuvrable vessels, able to dart into and out from our narrow fjords. But in this particular case, in Hafrsfjord, it was nothing short of brilliant to risk everything on one single raft holding several thousand armed men, once more a demonstration of Harald's tactical skills.

The fact that this resulted in vast areas round Stavanger losing all the trees may be regrettable, but one single kingdom with not all that much forest was – and probably is – much better than many little kingdoms with plenty of forest. SOMETHING HAS TO BE SACRIFICED TO UNITE THE MOTHERLAND!

King Harald is gathering the raft, having room for several thousand men, before the important battle in Hafrsfjord.

heard. Add one big king, wanting to become even bigger, and 31 small kings, not merely wanting to remain small, but absolutely determined to prevent the first one from getting bigger, or preferably to eliminate him for ever – and you have the recipe for The Battle of the Millennium.

It is said that arrows and spears flew hither and thither in such vast quantities that the sun was nearly blacked out – partly to the annoyance of some of the sunbathers ashore, making them move away from the shoreline and up on some rocks to get back into the sun – and the din of battle was so deafening that it could be heard all over Jæren. And you don't walk round Jæren in one day.

Those not directly involved flocked quickly to the fjord, that is, those who weren't there already, anxious to see what it was all about (remember there were no newspapers, radio, or TV in those days, and many were totally unaware of the historic event taken place in their area). Before long the crowd was standing so deep that those right at the back, not being able to see a thing and therefore not knowing what was going on, started sharpening their swords and axes, just to be on the safe side. You never knew in those days...

After the agreed 32 rounds, and after the parties had managed to untangle themselves and sort out who was still alive, and who was not, there was no doubt whatever that the 31 had been soundly and decisively beaten by Harald. Had the battle taken place ashore, the appropriate term would have been 'Beaten into the dust' – which would have been a remarkable deed indeed, seeing the battle took place on water.

Still, Harald was victorious, bordering on having obliterated the entire opposition. He had removed the very last obstacle for fulfilling his Great Calling and task in life. From that very day our country has been one, single, and United Kingdom. A truly magnificent victory, and an historic milestone without equal in our history. Little wonder that the name of the place, and the year, are two of the otherwise very few names/dates the average Norwegian ever remembers from the history lessons at school: 'Hafrsfjord' and '872'. ('872' must not be confused with the postal code for Hafrsfjord, which is 4045).

Immediately following the battle it was decided to erect a memorial or statue to commemorate the occasion for ever, just to make sure no Norwegian ever forgot what had just taken place, and some stones were quickly sculpted, signifying the 31 little kings and the one Big King. It was decided to place these on the spot where the battle had taken place, but it would seem that in the sheer excitement of all that had happened, no one left a thought to the fact that it is extremely difficult to erect some stone pillars on water – *and make them stay there.*

However, such a grand victory required that a new set of stones was sculpted, and this time they decided to erect them as close to the site of the battle as possible, *but ashore.* A wise decision, and they can be seen there to this day, right on the water's edge, reminding everyone passing by or stopping about the most significant moment in our country's history.

The day after this tremendous battle, King Harald went to the hairdresser, where – as his golden hair tumbled down in quantities – he uttered the now so famous words: 'Norway is well worth a haircut!'

As can be seen, Harald Hårfagre is far from a pretty sight, sitting on Norway's Throne. No wonder the family had to resort to falsifying history.

*Snorre, full name Snorre Sturlason (1178-1241). Icelandic Chieftain, historian and *skald*. Wrote extensively and meticulously about everything that took place; he is the major single source of everything we know about the Vikings and their way of life. Without him we would have nearly nothing.

It is very clear that the entire Harald-family have succeeded in their serious falsification of history with respect to Harald's long and fair hair. (True, they did so for the sake of a good cause). That hairs were cut after the victory in Hafrsfjord, is certain, but it is far from certain that these belonged to Harald. The truth is that Harald was born bald, and remained bald all his life. This is clearly evidenced by the linguistic tradition of the Norwegian language, always emphasizing what a person does not have. A person with only one eye is always known as 'He with the eye'. If he has only one leg, he is invariably called: 'He with the leg'; and someone without any hairs on his head will, of course, be called 'He with the hair' ('The fair haired' or similar). (This ancient custom is used without exception to this day in Norwegian politics: 'Høyre' (lit. 'Right'; i.e. The Conservatives) is in reality a party on the left. 'Arbeiderpartiet' (The Labour Party) is in reality a party for Big Business; 'Kristelig Folkeparti' (The Christian People's Party) is more or less the opposite, and 'Fremskrittspartiet' (the Progressive Party) is far from progressive.)

So – whose golden locks fell for the scissors in the year of our Lord 872? And who was the model for the false portrait of King Harald in Snorre?*

Did Harald have an hitherto unknown sister or brother who had to sacrifice her or his beautiful hair in order to unite the Kingdom? Whoever it was: THE SACRIFICE WAS NOT IN VAIN!

But Harald hadn't ruled the country for long before some became dissatisfied with the way he did things. This applied in particular to what we today would call 'the upper classes', the large landowners ('large' referring to the size of the land here, and not, of course, to the size of the owners), the various earls and chieftains scattered about, still in existence, albeit without any power or influence, and undoubtedly handfuls of others here and there. A direct reason for this was that one of the very first actions of King Harald when he emerged, hair cut, from the hairdresser, was to impose taxes. As a temporary measure, true, but still taxes. And he was quite strict in this respect; granting no concessions to married couples and/or people with children, making no distinction between someone with a mortgage and someone without. And what's more, *all* income was liable to tax, from the very first penny, irrespective.

Harald was no small king with small considerations, but then – he was Norway's first king – and many hoped he would also turn out to be the last. But these were bitterly disappointed, and the saga does not mention them again, so we have no idea what happened to them.

For a short while after that fateful year 872, a counter-revolution was looming just round the corner, but since those plotting such a dastardly deed did not manage to get any support from any foreign powers – not even Sweden or Denmark – their scheming collapsed and so did they.

With no hope of getting rid of Harald, those opposed to him (and remember these included many of the more important and wealthier sections of society), started leaving the country, much in the same way as the Pilgrim Fathers and, later, the Irish during the potato famine, would do all those many years later. Like the Pilgrim Fathers and the Irish, they headed west and – in their particular case – settled in Iceland and Greenland, with the odd one heading straight across the Atlantic to America (see *Leif Eiriksson*). The question is then whether the fact that so many splendid men and women left the country was an advantage or a drawback for the country as a whole. The answer is that it was probably both.

The **drawback** was that it was mainly the country's top people who packed their belongings, stuffed the boats full of family members, and headed west, never to come back again. True, many of them might well have written a letter or two, but since we don't know this for certain, we won't speculate any further.

The **advantage** (and many are those who are adamant that this outweighed the drawback by a very wide margin) was that it was this very emigration which laid the foundation stone for what we may rightly call The Norwegian Empire (more details later in the book). It is from this period of our country's history we have the saying: 'It's an ill wind that blows no good'. This is really a corruption of one of the many superb poems (lays) from the hands of one of the *skalds*, the first part of which reads as follows in translation:

> Ill it may seem, the wind which blows
> the splendid ships across the Seas.
> But better times and better places
> they seek and find who set the sails.

This was regarded as a particularly beautiful and mighty lay, and the *skald* received great ovations and much praise. Shortly after that, the *skald* left the country himself, destination uncertain, and we don't hear any more from or about him. Harald Hårfagre reigned supreme for about 40 years, and when he died, his youngest son, Håkon, who was being educated in England in the care of the English King, Adalstein, was called home to take over. And so he did.

This brings us to:

B: HÅKON DEN GODE (HÅKON THE GOOD)

Håkon den Gode was a good King – hence the name.

As mentioned already: Håkon received his education in England, whether it was at Oxford or Cambridge, we don't know, but the mere fact that he bothered to go to school was a good sign, there were plenty of kings, queens, and other such elevated personages who could hardly read and write, so Håkon set a good example.

The question as to exactly which University King Håkon attended will probably never be answered, but we do know that this good, kind, and peaceful king was quite a sportsman; this is very obvious from the way he handled his very sharp sword **Kvernbit** *(literally 'Millstone-bite').*

But what is not known by many in the UK, or even in Norway for that matter, is that it was Håkon den Gode who started the now so famous and annual Boat Race: The Vikings had for decades rowed up the Thames, against both wind and current, to attack, rob, and sack London. When doing so, every ship competed against the others, all wanting to be first and thus have the richest pickings. Håkon didn't like all this burning and sacking, being a peaceful man, but realising it would be very difficult indeed to stop all this rowing on the Thames, racing against each other, he thought of a way of turning it into a more peaceful pursuit, and talked some of his fellow students at the University into a rowing-competition on the Thames.

During these very first years only one team started, and it won more and more convincingly every year. And the cup, 'Kvernbit Cup'; or only 'Kvernbit' for short, was won outright by the most eminent oarsman of them all, namely our very own King Håkon.

Great celebration as King Håkon receives **Kvernbit** *from the English king after having won three out of two possible victories at the annual Boat Race.*

A miscreant heading for the seabed, with a millstone round his neck. (This picture is from before Håkon den Gode's time.)

When his father, Harald Hårfagre, died, Håkon den Gode was summoned home to Norway to take over ruling the country. This was not as easy as it might sound, and without going into details, a very brief explanation will show why: Harald Hårfagre had married a Danish princess – probably because there weren't all that many Norwegian princesses available on the open market – and they had a son called Eirik. He soon earned the nickname 'Blodøks' (Blood Axe), which should amply describe the sort of fellow Håkon the Good was up against. And up against he was, since Eirik – and later his sons, known as 'Eiriksønnene' (Sons of Eirik) – and with equally bloody axes, claimed Norway as theirs as well. A family feud if ever there was one.

Anyway, before Håkon left England he received the '*Kvernbit Cup*' – or just '*Kvernbit*' – from the English king (see illustration). This was a sword which was so strong and sharp that it could split a millstone in two, and a more logical name than '*Kvernbit*' (Millstone-bite) would be hard to find. We do not know with certainty today what Håkon wanted two half millstones for, but some historians are of the opinion that in England, already in these early days, they had what we would call rough ground and fine ground flour, and that the half millstones served the former purpose. But we don't know this for certain. What, however, we DO know for certain is that Håkon never left home without *Kvernbit*, just in case he should happen to come across a farmer or anyone else who wanted a millstone cut into two. Håkon was that sort of king.

> *It is probably thanks to Håkon den Gode that the inhuman form of punishment, 'a millstone round the neck', was abolished. By splitting millstones into two, he killed two birds with one stone: the population got both coarse ground and finely ground flour for baking bread, at the same time, anyone being unfortunate enough to get the other half of the millstone round his neck and thrown into deep water, could easily wriggle out of it, get loose – and survive. The result was that this form for punishment died out which meant that Håkon was described as 'the Good' even by miscreants who had deserved a worse fate. Somewhat later, this method of execution was copied by the Mafia, but with a more modern touch: with concrete round the legs, allegedly a more humane method.*

The reason why Håkon was a peaceful king who did not much like fighting and conflicts, was that he had been introduced to Christianity whilst in England (Church of England). So he preferred to keep the Sunday holy and refrain from rushing around chopping people's heads off, much to the disappointment of most of his men. But the calendar they had at that time was a rather unreliable affair, so the days and dates were easily muddled up – with the result that there was sometimes space for a little raid or a fight even on a Sunday. And Håkon's men preferred to keep it that way.

We have already mentioned the terrible sons, of that dreadful man, Eirik Bloodaxe. They had travelled to Denmark to seek the help of the King of Denmark in pushing Håkon into oblivion so they could take over the country themselves.

Their men didn't think much of them going to Denmark – they felt they should have stayed home and kept the language pure and their axes red. But Eiriksønnene did not agree, and many are those who say that by doing what they did, they sowed the seeds for the language conflict we have in Norway today. Whether this is correct or not, is a different matter.

The Danish king expressed his willingness to help these Sons of Eirik in their attempt to lift their uncle off the Norwegian throne and plonk themselves onto it in his place, and – like the Spanish Armada years later – they set sail, heading North. But different from the Armada, which sailed and failed only once, these Sons kept sailing and failing, time and again. Every time they tried to land and get a foothold in Norway, Håkon and his men soon sent them packing southwards again, so decisively and frequently that one can only marvel at their ability to learn little or nothing. And each time this happened, Håkon's *skalds* reeled off more and more lays, each lay more flowery and near-hysterical in its praise of the King than the one before. In the end it was nearly too much even for the King himself:

> The King killed many foes,
> drove the Danes down to Denmark,
> never did we see the Danes
> dart so dervishly* back home.
> The Sons of Eirik scuttled South,
> their blood running red in their veins.
> Norse they are like the King himself,
> but the King beat them, boats and all.

And yet they kept on coming, aided and abetted by the King of Denmark, who probably hoped to get his hands on a fair slice of Norway himself (which, in fact, his successors did, some 500 or so years later when they got all of it). One day it so happened that Håkon was at his weekend retreat with most of his men just south of Bergen. Which was quite clever, really, since Bergen had not been founded yet, and maybe the reason why he did not stay in the city itself.

Anyway: they were all seated round the table when a man rushed in with such speed that although *he* stopped before he reached the King, his coat of mail didn't, and after having staggered to his feet and helped up those around him who were all knocked down at the same time, he managed to splutter that the visible part of the North Sea was full to the horizon of Sons of Eirik, Danes, and other riffraff. Different from that chap Pheidippides, who ran all the way from Marathon to Athens to inform his Emperor about the victory, only to drop dead as soon as he had delivered the happy message, this stout Viking regained his breath, took up arms and Reported for Duty.

Håkon called his *hird*† and all other able-bodied men immediately, and they all marched down onto the rocks by water's edge to receive the visitors in the proper manner. The King himself led the way, firing his arrows in the way it becomes a king, now and then giving *Kvernbit* a twirl or two in case there should happen to be someone close by wanting a millstone split in two.

Since Håkon had not expected any disturbance out there at his weekend retreat, in the middle of

---

*The meaning of the word 'dervishly' in this context is not known. But that does not in any way detract from the mighty quality of this lay. The *skald* refers both to the fact that the Sons of Eirik were Norwegian, and therefore more courageous and tougher than the Danes, as well as to the fact that they were sons of Eirik Bloodaxe, without actually *saying* so in clear language. – A truly masterful lay. The *skald* is, unfortunately, completely unknown.

†Hird' is described as 'household, King's Court, guard', but was really more than that: they were hand-picked, specially trusted men, sworn to defend their King with their own lives. The best of the lot.

a jolly good party, he had his helmet of pure gold on, and as he stood there, right in front of all his brave men, all firing arrows and chopping with their swords as best they could (and that was pretty good), the sun came out for a brief moment, some of the rays being reflected by Håkon's helmet, making him as visible as a lighthouse at work on a dark night.*

Realising what an excellent target his king was, one of his men was quick-thinking enough to throw a piece of cloth† over the helmet. As soon as the reflection disappeared, making King Håkon blend into the background, one of the Sons of Eirik shouted mockingly: 'What's happened to the King of the Norsemen – is he hiding, or where did the Golden Helmet disappear to?' Håkon grabbed a corner of the cloth and with one strong movement pulled it off the helmet, at the same time he shouted back, equally loud or even louder, seeing he was a king: 'Just keep a steady course, Eiriksson, and you'll find the King of the Norsemen!'

And the Son of Eirik did – he kept a steady course and one of his arrows found King Håkon in the arm, just below the shoulder. Once more, Håkon's men succeeded in beating back the Sons of Eirik and all the Danes, making them set sail for Denmark for the umpteenth time, but they did not succeed in saving Håkon's life. He asked them to row him to Hellen, not that far away, since he was born there. They did as requested, and not long after arriving there, the king died where he was born. The whole country grieved, because everyone agreed he had been a Good King.

See more details next page:

---

*There is no substance in the rumour that it was this incident which gave some of those present the idea of forming the Norwegian Association of Lighthouse Keepers shortly afterwards.

†The saga describes it as a 'hat or a hood', without saying who would walk round with a hat or a hood at the ready. Bearing in mind the circumstances (partying, eating/drinking, relaxation, cooking), it is more likely that what was thrown over the King's helmet was a tea towel or similar. Within a very short time, this simple idea to use a tea-towel to protect your head against strong sunshine was taken up by people living in warmer countries (Arabs, Palestinians etc.), and is now a well-established custom, in all likelihood without any of them realising exactly *where* this no doubt efficient habit has its roots!

Here follow the details promised on the previous page:

The author is touching on something important when he hints that the 'hat' mentioned by the saga about Håkon den Gode and his golden helmet, in reality was a tea towel or similar.

We see quite clearly that the cloth being thrown over the King's helmet has a pattern (arabesque), which we recognise has being the same as the pattern seen on textiles belonging to the Caliph the Splendid's dream palace in Damascus.

Exactly HOW this damask came to be there in the first place is nothing short of a mystery which has never been explained in a satisfactory way. Nor has it been explained HOW this one incident – with one of King Håkon's men throwing the cloth over the King's helmet – resulted in whole nations much further south taking up this habit of walking round with what looks like tea-towels on their heads. Perhaps King Håkon had Arab mercenaries in his army and they thought it was an old custom in Norway, copying it and spreading it when they got back home?

It is a fascinating thought...

A well-meaning cook has just flung a cloth over King Håkon's head. As we see, there can be no doubt that the pattern is a genuine arabesque. But we see equally clearly that the cloth makes it extremely difficult for King Håkon to take proper aim. In this way, the cloth, meant for protection, contributed to the fall of The Good King!

(THIS PAGE IS BLANK

IN MEMORY OF

HÅKON DEN GODE)

It would appear that the entire episode was based on a terrible misunderstanding: when Olav referred to a dog which, in addition to being a dog was also a heathen, and with which he had little or no desire to enter into matrimony, he clearly thought of the German SCHWEINEHUND which he had caught a glimpse of the time he passed Northern Germany on his way to England.

This awful sight made such an indelible impression on him that the mere thought of marrying such a beast made him climb right up to the top of a very high stone column in the centre of what is now called Trondheim (in those days it was Nidaros) to be well clear of the ground. He can be seen there to this day.

C: OLAV TRYGVASSON

Olav was son of Trygve, hence the name.

He was a very capable king, and just like Håkon den Gode, he was also a Christian, (the English king was his Godfather), and he wanted to christen all of the country, but for all his efforts he only managed to convert the coastal areas.

It is nevertheless possible he might have reached the aim he set himself if only he had lived a bit longer than he did. But he didn't: he died in an ambush quite young (see Index). All because of a woman.

It was leap year, and she had proposed to Olav. Not only was he a king, he was in addition a tall, handsome man with clean features – that is, what features one could discern amongst all the hair and beard – the type of man over whom women swoon, breathe faster and feel faint the moment they set eyes on him. But Olav was an upright, honest, and not least courageous man, and replied that he most certainly did not want a dog of a heathen for a

King Olav sees a German Schweinehund. No wonder he sought refuge high up and far away!

wife. She did not like the answer, in fact, she got livid, saying, as she turned on her heels and marched away: 'This might well be the finish of you!'

The tragic result of this totally unnecessary misunderstanding was that when Olav sailed south to Germany on holiday the following year, the woman whose hand he had refused, let's face it, in rather a blunt manner (showing clearly that Olav was no politician, or he would have wrapped his reply up in about 500 words, carefully chosen in such a way that it would have taken the lady in question about three years to sort out what he meant – and even then she wouldn't have been sure), she joined forces with some of Olav's enemies, determined to get her own back.

They were fully aware that to meet Olav in open battle, face to face, would be suicide, so they laid in wait at Svolder, not far from Germany, where there is a narrow sound through which Olav had to sail on his way home. And a narrow sound is, as we know, just the place for an ambush. And that's exactly what happened.

Olav had, as was customary, despatched his smaller and faster ships ('corvettes' and 'destroyers' we would have called them today) to sail ahead to find a suitable place to anchor or Christen for the night, whilst he himself and some of his men followed in the slower, but superb *Ormen Lange* – according to the saga one of the most magnificent Viking ships ever built.

His enemies let all the smaller ships unhindered through – it was Olav, and Olav only, they were interested in. So when Olav and his men, relaxing and sunbathing and probably drinking a hornful or two of mead (apart from the Watch, that is) onboard the *Ormen Lange*, entered the sound, 'enemy', 'risk', and 'danger' would probably be the last three words any of them would have had in mind. Little did they know...

The ambush was a total success seen from the ambushers' side; less so, seen from Olav's side. Olav was killed, and many of his men with him, but some were spared, since neither that scorned woman, nor any of her cowardly helpers, had anything against anyone but Olav. Amongst those spared was – fortunately for posterity – the young *skald* and archer, Einar Tamberskjelve, the courageous one mentioned earlier in this narrative, whose bow was hit by an arrow, and then – finally – told the king that the king's bow wasn't strong enough – remember?

'Fortunately', because he went on to serve the next king well as well, and produced many a good lay after the Battle at Svolder.

Whilst all this was going on in that narrow sound, the vanguard of Olav's ships and men had indeed found a most suitable place to anchor, and having dropped the number of anchors necessary, they settled down, mead horn in hands, waiting for their king and that splendid *Ormen Lange*, leaving one man up front as look-out – just in case.

As darkness fell, and no Olav appeared, a certain unease amongst the men became noticeable, but they assumed that their king had decided that it might be risky business to navigate such a large vessel in narrow, unknown and mostly uncharted waters, and had therefore pulled in somewhere for the night, waiting for daylight. With that they all bedded down, leaving one man as look-out. Just in case.

Next morning came, with bright sunshine and a fair wind blowing from the south, so they expected *Ormen Lange* and King Olav any moment. Came midday, with the sun high in the sky, and no Olav, they became very worried indeed, realising that something terrible had happened. That's when the *skald* got up, standing in the middle of one of the smallest ships, speaking gently and softly – yet clear enough for them all to hear his beautiful, yet sad, words – it was as if he knew exactly what had happened:

> When we woke,
> anxiously awaiting all the rest,
> Olav, our king, and *Ormen Lange*,
> nowhere to be seen, but nowhere.
> All asking after our king.
> The sea, empty of sails, full of silence,
> Silence – sadness – sorrow –
> we set sail again, sailing North to Norway,
> the wet waves washing over our king's grave.
> We shall miss him more than most.

They all fell as silent as the sea when the *skald* had uttered these words, and for all every man present thought this was a particularly moving, poignant, and very beautiful lay, he received not a single word of praise or recognition. Somehow it did not appear to be right to hand out ovations at a time like this.

As mentioned already: this incident took place in the year 1000, and is therefore extremely easy to remember.

Olav Trygvasson was a truly Great Viking, an athlete of dimensions, and a very good king. The saga tells us that he used to walk on the oars as his men rowed the boats – something which probably seemed as odd in those days as it does to us today. There is, unfortunately, not a single lay which may explain WHY Olav kept walking on the oars when his men rowed. Some theories have been advanced, but since one is no more convincing than any of the others, there is no point in delving deeper into this question, apart from saying that the one theory that MAY possibly be pointing us in the right direction is the one saying that Olav did it to keep in shape. Some sort of physical exercise in other words. Whatever – it does indeed seem a very strange thing to do. But he did it very well, according to the saga. So let's leave it at that.

Since Olav had been a rather popular king, it was decided to have a nationwide collection with the aim of having a statue made of him. At first, the intention – as expressed by the Organising Committee – was to erect this statue where King Olav had been so cowardly ambushed, but then someone remembered what happened to the first statues, erected just over a hundred years earlier, to commemorate the famous Battle of Hafrsfjord, and that idea was abandoned, and it was instead, for some reason or the other, decided to put it up in Nidaros (Trondheim). Where it stands to this day. Very high up.

D: OLAV HARALDSSON DEN HELLIGE (OLAV HARALDSSON THE HOLY)

This Olav is a king towering high in our history – one of the largest personalities who has ever sat on our throne. When he lived, he was also called Olav den Digre (Olav the Big One). But the nickname by which he became, and is, most famous, and the one he preferred, was Den Hellige (The Holy). He got this because he succeeded in converting the remainder of the country and thus the people to Christianity, and he is therefore regarded as the founder of the Norwegian State Church, or Church of Norway. He was a genuine Christian, which is also apparent from the fact that he and his men always entered into battle under the war cry: 'Forward Christians, Royal soldiers, bearers of the Cross!' It is difficult to be more Christian than that.

Olav was determined to convert those not yet converted to Christianity even before he ascended to the throne. And the very first thing he did after he had come to power, was to zig-zag the country, spreading the good word, arranging 'baptism-meetings', as he called them.

But for all his persuasive powers, it was not all that easy. Most of the Vikings were quite happy, in fact more than happy, with their old Gods, with Odin right on top, followed by Thor and all the other well-known and highly respected divine figures, and could see no reason for or benefit from discarding these old faithfuls in favour of a totally unknown foreign fellow who didn't even speak Norwegian. And they said so. But like any decent authority, Olav knew what was best for them, and he had his own way of persuading them by giving them a totally free choice: beheading or baptism. Naturally, most chose baptism, which was done on the spot, after which they were immediately released and declared to be Christians.

The saga gives us one concrete example of his persuasive powers, from such a meeting high up in the Gudbrands Valley, the long, long valley running more or less from Oslo to near enough Trondheim. Not quite, but near enough. He had called all men over the age of 12 to the meeting, and when he asked them to convert, they said no. No way. Absolutely no, they said. As with one voice. To put it simply: they refused.

Olav then took an axe which happened to be nearby and smashed the idols they had been sacrificing food and all sorts of goodies too, and out jumped toads, frogs, snakes (the saga does not, unfortunately, describe in more detail how snakes jump), and he asked if THESE were the Gods they had been putting their faith in. They had to admit that, well – yes, it might seem a bit odd, but...

Like one man, they chose baptism rather than beheading, but they didn't like it, not one little bit, and never quite forgave Olav. Carrying on like that, it was only a question of time before he had amassed so many enemies that things got serious. And time did not stand still: before too long he had to flee to Sweden (numerous good Norwegians were to follow his example about 910 years later), but since he was a king he was not interned, and became a good friend of the King of Sweden instead. The King of Sweden thought it was pretty bad that his friend and neighbour should lose his kingdom, so he helped him by supplying him with men and equipment to form an army.

After some proper training, Olav crossed the border back into Norway, firmly determined to teach his countrymen a lesson they wouldn't forget in a hurry. But there were many of them, and his friend, the King of Sweden, warned him that for all the Norwegians were basically a rum lot, he would not find the task an easy one. The year was 1030.

Crossing the border back into Norway with his army, he was enthusiastically greeted in the sparsely populated border-areas since he had many more men than anyone there could rustle together, and they all joined him, swelling his ranks. In those days, the County of Trøndelag (say, Trondheim and surrounding areas, roughly half way up Norway), was – for some reason – regarded as the most important part of the whole country. Olav thought that if he could conquer it, or – even better – get the *trønders* (the people living in Trøndelag) – on his side, he was more than half-way there. The *skald* put it like this:

> Olav, the king, marched his men
> menacingly many miles over the mountains.
> Wondering what would happen –
> wooing or war?*

King Olav was so impressed that the *skald*, as one of the very, very few, was permitted to grow a beard AND keep his hair.

The people of Trøndelag didn't think all that highly of Olav, so when he arranged for a meeting they attended in great numbers and equally great excitement, and all in a rather bad mood. Olav wanted negotiation, not confrontation, but he had made an extremely bad choice in this respect. The *trønders* speak a most peculiar dialect, virtually incomprehensible to anyone from outside the county (and Olav came from miles away) – the people born and living here are probably one of the exceedingly few groups of people in the world (perhaps the only one) who manage to keep what appears to be a sensible and normal conversation without the use of a single consonant. It does, admittedly, not sound like a conversation at all if you are not from these parts, but since the person being conversed to always seems to react in an obviously correct manner (smiling, nodding, shaking of head etc.) – AND giving a reply which meets with the same appropriate reaction, it is fair to assume they understand each other. But Olav didn't.

The *trønders* might well, for all Olav and the saga knew, have agreed to every single word he said, but since Olav and his men had no way of telling (remember a fair number of his men were Swedes!) – he broke off the negotiations and let his trumpeters blow the signal for battle. The saga relates that the trumpeters blew so hard and long that three of them had to be excused any further service for the next two months.

The two armies clashed at a place called Stiklestad, probably because it had such a convenient situation, just outside Trondheim – or Nidaros as the city was called then. The army opposed to

---

*This excellent and very expressive lay crossed the North Sea somehow, and appeared later in Great Britain in the version of a Duke of York who marched his 10,000 men up a hill and down again – probably because he either changed his mind or – different from Olav – didn't know what he was doing.

Olav was called *Bondehæren* (lit. 'Army of Farmers'), because it consisted mainly of farmers. So did Olav's army but his was not, for some inexplicable reason, called *Bondehæren*. Perhaps it was done like that to avoid confusion.

This battle – the Battle at Stiklestad in 1030 – is one of the most controversial battles in our long and proud history. Numerous researchers, historians, and know-alls say that the only reason why Olav lost, was that he himself had no real military training, having spent by far the most of his time rushing about, chopping up idols and converting people. A few battles, here and there, indeed – but no REAL, old-fashioned giant clash with anybody. Until now.

Others are equally convinced that the one and only reason why Olav lost, was that his army was riddled with Swedes. And when, pray, did a Swede beat a Norwegian in a genuine fight? Olav's mistake was not so much fleeing to Sweden to rest for a while – his giant blunder was to rely on Swedes to help him beat his fellow Norwegians. You might as well try and conquer Russia with 5 men.

It is impossible for us, here and now, to decide who is nearest to the truth, but if we look coolly at the situation and analyse all known facts, there can be no doubt that Olav dropped a clanger when he let the battle take place ashore, on land. If he, like his predecessor Harald Hårfagre, had arrived by ship, and thus forced the Army of Farmers to come and meet him out in the Trondheim Fjord, it is more than likely that he would have won. As it was, he was killed, leaning against a huge boulder after having been wounded, and it is patently impossible to lean against a big boulder in the middle of a fjord. But he lost the battle, and was – as mentioned – killed by a spear whilst leaning against a boulder.

The date of this battle is very important: 29th July, 1030. Important, because if you get the date wrong, you end up by celebrating *Olsok* (St. Olav's Day) on the wrong date. That can be very embarrassing.

It is from this memorable battle we have a very famous Norwegian poem, written much later, saying something like that what is best and most excellent in this life is not so much living as such, but to leave something behind when you finally go. 'A mark', as the poet so vividly expressed it. What the poet had in mind and referred to, was Olav's famous standard-bearer, *Trond Foleson* – as famous in Norwegian history as David Crocket is in the US of A, Grace Darling in England, and Robert the Bruce in Scotland. When the battle raged at its worst, Trond did not falter, but carried Olav's standard high and straight, for all to see and the enemy to fear. Having to hold it with both hands there was little, if anything, he could do to defend himself. When he was fatally wounded by an arrow, he used his last and rapidly fading strength to ram the standard hard into the ground, gasping with his last breath: 'The King's standard shall not fall, but remain!' Having said that, he died.

A *skald* who happened to be nearby saw and heard this brave and selfless action and recorded it on the spot for all eternity. It is this lay one of our nationally famous poets picked up again hundreds of years later and made into a most stirring, emotional, and swashbuckling poem. We all know it by heart.

There are several Norwegian words for 'standard', as meant here, and the poet settled for *merke* (lit. 'mark'), probably because of the double meaning, lifting the poem to even greater heights, as in 'leaving a mark', i.e. not disappearing without trace.

Again, when you read the illustrator's remarks and see the illustrations which follow, you will once more realise that he has, unfortunately, looked up the wrong meaning in English, but it is nevertheless included here due to its artistic, NOT historic, merits in this case.

The confusion arises because we have simply imported the English 'pins' – as in 'lapel pins', straight into our language, and many now use this instead of the real Norwegian *merke*. So, with that little explanation:

> *Whilst the armies are getting ready for the decisive battle, Trond Foleson has erected his stall with his 'marks' (pins), hoping to make a fair amount of money on selling 'Olav-pins'. Some hope! Trond fell two hours later, but a nearby skald (on the right) made the incident immortal by his famous lay '... by leaving a mark behind you'.*

Olav was buried shortly after the battle, but some time later he was exhumed (the exact, or even approximate, reason for this is not known), and when it was found that his hair and nails had grown, he was declared a Saint. Sceptics still think he was buried alive.

Strangely enough, bearing in mind the tremendous significance of this battle, we have no lays from it, apart from the one already mentioned – in spite of the fact that we know there were many *skalds* present. We know this from the saga which tells us that they were extremely busy, laying like no *skalds* had ever layed before, running from one side to the other, shuttling in between the fighting hordes, being everywhere all the time, many losing their voices completely, having to withdraw since a *skald* with no voice is about as useful as a *berserk* with no arms. The saga finishes by saying that 'Never in living memory have so few layed so much for so many.'

It is indeed regrettable that – apart from the one lay already mentioned – the rest would appear to have been lost for ever. This is a pity since it is fairly safe to assume that the *skalds* really came up with some excellent lays which would have impressed us greatly to this very day.

> *But thanks to Trond Foleson, Olav's standard-bearer during at least most of the Battle at Stiklestad, the carrying of 'marks; or 'pins', became popular to the extreme. Landowner and smallholder, berserk and skald, all started to wear pins of all sorts of shapes and sizes in the hope of leaving a mark (pin) behind should they happen to suddenly fall. It was no more than a hope for the vast majority, since during a fall it is only too easy for all the marks – or pins – to tumble with you. How hopeless it all was is clear from the simple fact that so far we have not found one single pin from any of them!*

*An example of a Viking from **Romsdalen**, falling off a steep cliff. As we see, all his marks (pins) are falling with him, disappearing into oblivion without trace.*

E: HARALD HÅRDRÅDE (HARALD THE HARD RULER)

arald wasn't christened Hårdråde – on the contrary; his proper name was Harald III Sigurdsson, because he was son of Sigurd. But he was most certainly a real, genuine Viking king, through and through: at the tender age of 15 years he took part in the Battle at Stiklestad on Olav's side, and he managed to escape being a POW when Olav lost the battle. That escape was the start of a truly eventful life, even for a Viking.

He started it by travelling across Europe. With no passport, no entry visa of any sort, no cars, trains, buses or even bicycles, indeed, no roads as we know them, this was no mean feat at all. He had to walk, or ride if he was lucky. There were no B & B or hotels anywhere, the YHA hadn't even been thought of, and it was anything but easy to get work along the way, work, that is, suitable for a man whose veins were running full of royal blood. The one and only way he managed to sustain himself and the faithful men who accompanied him, was by doing the odd job, sacking and robbing here and there.

He must have been pretty successful at this since he ended up as far south as Turkey. And that's a long way from Norway, even today. (Some are of the opinion that Harald arrived in Turkey by mistake, taking the wrong turn somewhere along the route; he *had* intended working his way down to Spain, to Costa del Sol, settling there for a while, but since this is a flimsy theory built on the purest speculation, we won't even mention it here.)

Whatever – he entered into the service of the Turkish Emperor, who put him in charge of a gang of Norse Vikings operating under the name of *Væringene*. This rather strange name comes from *varing* – someone who has sworn an oath of allegiance to a king, or emperor, or whoever. In this case an emperor, no less.

You may well wonder why on earth a Viking king, with all his faithful men, should enter into the service of someone from Turkey – emperor or not. And well you may – it had all had to do with the Swedes.

We have already mentioned that the Vikings from Norway and Denmark mostly sailed west, veering to the south now and then. But *Vesterveg* was their favourite; a more or less natural direction for anyone setting sail from those countries. Realising that three could rob, rape, and plunder more than two – albeit you then had to split the loot into three, and not two – the Danes and the Norwegians invited the Swedes to join them. A rare occurrence, really, since the three of them spent a great deal of their time fighting each other.

A quick glance at a map covering that part of the world makes it clear that all a Dane and/or a Norwegian has to do in order to head for Britain or thereabouts, is simply to embark, hoist the sail, and weigh anchor. It will be close to a miracle if you don't hit Anglo-Saxon land. However, if you are a Swede, things are vastly different. And this is where things got utterly confused: fully aware that the Swedes were different from themselves, the Danes and the Norwegians enclosed clear and very detailed instructions with the invitation as to how to find them in order to join in before they all sailed across the North Sea. Assuming that the majority of the Swedish fleet would start from Stockholm, the instructions were to turn starboard and out the Baltic, then starboard again and squeeze between Sweden and Denmark, carry on with Denmark on port side, and then sharp port and round the tip of Jutland – and there you are! They might well have added a 'You can't miss it!', the Saga doesn't say.

But they did. Miss it, that is. It is fairly general knowledge that the Swedes, as the one and only nation in Scandinavia, kept to the left on the roads – with everyone else keeping to the right. With hindsight it is therefore easy to say that they probably had the same rules at sea (nobody seems to know for certain), with an inherent risk of mixing up 'starboard' and 'port'. AND THAT IS EXACTLY WHAT HAPPENED – with far-reaching consequences to this day.

With a fair wind behind them, the Swedish fleet left Stockholm behind – and turned PORT instead of starboard, thus sailing UP the Baltic, and not DOWN. At the point where they thought the invitation told them to turn starboard, they did so, but due to their first error they did not enter Kattegat, but a long and winding river, leading them deep and far into what is now Russia. This confused them a bit to start with, but then they thought the Danes and the Norwegians might be just round the next bend, and carried on.

Needless to say, they never found them, but having gone that far the Swedes decided to go it alone, did some plunder and pillage along the route, followed various winding rivers, only to end up in the Black Sea. At this stage they began to realise that they had taken the wrong turn somewhere, but since it was a long way back – not least having to row AGAINST the river currents, they settled for raiding Istanbul, or Constantinople as it was then. The Vikings called it Miklagard, a far more pronounceable name if you were a Viking, but also for another and even better reason: if or when you come back home to your wife after an absence of a year or two, and she asks weren't you meant to just nip across to England and bring some goodies home, and where the hell have you been all this time? – it would hardly do just to say 'Constantinople'. She might easily take that to be the name of a woman, and you WOULD be in trouble, tough Viking or not! But if you said 'Miklagard!', she might ask you a few more questions, but that would probably be all.

And this is where Harald and his men come into the picture: the Emperor, residing in Constantinople (or Miklagard), was no fool, unlike the one with the new clothes. Instead of spending Turkish lives on fighting the Swedes, he had the brilliant idea of importing some Norwegians and Danes to do the job for him! And as Harald happened to be around, the Emperor asked him, promised him some Turkish delights of various sorts – and that was it.

So successful were King Harald (well, as yet, he was not a king, of course, only full of royal blood, but still) and his men, that their escapades all round the Mediterranean countries made them so feared in the area that children who misbehaved to the extent that they started sliding out of parental control were often told that 'If you don't behave, the *væringene* will come and get you!' This was normally more than enough to make even the most obstreperous child behave beautifully for the next six weeks or so.

Because of their robust behaviour* they became very popular with the Turkish Emperor, who showered them with gifts of many types. And it is from Harald that we have a saying in use to this day whenever we don't understand a single word: even the Emperor felt that these Norse warriors overdid it slightly at times, but whenever he asked Harald to tone it down, just a little bit, Harald shook his head and said: 'I haven't the faintest idea what the chap is on about – it's all Greek† to me!'

Harald's Turkish venture very nearly ended in complete disaster: he was silly enough to have an affair with the Empress Zoe. Silly, since history is crowded with examples of what happens to people who have affairs with empresses, queens, and such-like. He and some of his men ended up in prison, charged with an offence which carried the capital punishment: being an enemy of the people.††

Fortunately, he and those imprisoned with him managed to escape and find their way back to Norway, where Harald became king and ruled for many years – 'too many' according to some. With his urge to travel he was rarely at home, spending most of his time abroad, fighting, pillaging, sacking, burning, raping. Indeed, he won so many battles, fights, and skirmishes that within two years of becoming king he was 18 points clear on top of the Premier Sacking League.

> *Here it is necessary to make a slight correction to the otherwise so factually correct and well-informed author.*
>
> *Far from 'having an affair' with Empress Zoe, it was Empress Zoe **who had an affair with Harald!** AND THAT IS A QUITE DIFFERENT MATTER!*
>
> *She was young and frisky. The young and handsome Norseman in charge of her husband's **Væringer** could not speak Turkish and could therefore neither speak to her nor understand what she wanted to tell him. So there was only one way she could tell – or show – him what she meant! (He was not called the Hard Ruler for nothing). We should keep the facts straight!*

*So robust, in fact, that the troubles they caused are noticeable in this area to this day.
†'Greek' or 'Turkish': what's the difference to Viking ears?
††Due to this, Harald has given us another famous saying. as much used today as it was then: 'Ingratitude is the world's reward!'.

One year Harald decided to sail in *Vesterveg* like his ancestors (to date he had mainly journeyed south, straying a bit east now and then). At first all went well. He came as a complete and not very welcome surprise on the English, most of them watching cricket and thus having their minds on more serious things than possible attacks by vile foreigners.

True to their habit of not doing much until they have their backs to the wall, the English gradually recovered, gathered an army and marched to repel the attack. The two armies met at Stamford Bridge in the historic year 1066 (again the Vikings started something: battles are often still being fought there in the football season to this day). It was a tremendous battle – so tremendous that it has forever after been called The Battle of Britain.

For a long time it looked as if Harald – the Norwegian Harald (to complicate matters the English king was also called Harald – or Harold, they weren't all that fussy about the exact spelling in those days) would win; at one stage he was leading at least 4-0, when he was hit by an arrow in the throat and died. When his men saw their king fall, they dropped everything and rushed back to their ships as fast as helmets and chain-mail permitted, jumped onboard, hoisted the sails in great hurry and disappeared over the horizon.

The *skald* uttered quite a few lays, but since everyone present did not like the incident very much, the *skald* was seized and thrown overboard. What happened to him after that is unknown.

The fleeing Vikings were not pursued by the winning team since news had reached Harold – the English one – that the untrustworthy French had seized the opportunity, with the English in the middle of a match at Stamford Bridge, to land some forces in the South, near a place most suitably called Battle, hoping to beat them for once by falling on them in the back.

So Harold – still the English one – saw no reason at all to chase the Vikings any further, but quickly marched south to meet this new challenge and throw the garlic-eating French back to whence they came. Or preferably further, if at all possible. Unfortunately it wasn't, as we now all know – the tough fight against the Vikings, followed by a long march, was not the ideal preparation for the battle which followed.

So the French should be ever grateful to the Norwegians for making it possible for them to beat the English for once, albeit once only. We can only hope they are.

F: OLAV KYRRE (OLAV THE PEACEFUL)

It is no exaggeration to say that the Viking period, the real, lively, and genuine Viking period of which we are all so proud, goes down and out with Olav Kyrre. He was not a Viking king in the real sense – or in any sense for that matter; he was peaceful to the extreme, and was called *Kyrre* (The Peaceful One) before he had ruled for many days. He was the son of Harald Hårdråde – and it does not require all that vivid an imagination to imagine what Harald's reaction would have been had someone dared to call *him* 'Kyrre'!

So he shouldn't really be included here (we are, when all's said and done, talking about VIKING kings), but since he founded Bergen – or *Bjørgvin* as he named the city as he cut the red ribbon and declared it open and that it was to be Norway's capital – he warrants a mention, if nothing else.

It was no accident that he founded Bergen – on the contrary, it was only after careful studies, research, and serious contemplation he did so. And by doing so he hoped that a large majority of all strong and leading men, able and willing to bear arms, would move to his new capital and before long drown in all the incessant rain, whilst he himself sat relatively dry in his royal residence on a small hill just outside the city. High enough for him to keep is nose above all the water. In his opinion the best and only way to secure eternal peace in the country.

But the Frenchman Para Plui ruined Olav's Grand Plan by inventing the umbrella shortly afterwards, and Olav died in 1093, a wet, sad, and disappointed king. He was buried in Bergen, and it has been said that he turns twice in his grave every time the sun shines on Bergen. So, on the whole, he lies quite still. Those floating near him heard him utter a threat before disappearing

As we all know, the French inventor Para Plui (1045-1096), reached a relatively ripe old age by the standards of his day. And he lived long enough to see Olav Kyrre's hope for more peaceful times literally drying up because of his invention. Instead of drowning like rats (Rattus norvegicus), the belligerent inhabitants of Bergen became drier and drier, and more and more belligerent, due to the characteristics of the umbrella. This belligerence kept intact and unchanged for years and proved too much even for the combined English/Dutch fleet, hundreds of years later. It had to yield to the dry citizens in all the rain – the cannon ball above the door of Domkirken (The Cathedral in Bergen) and the many umbrella-shops bearing clear evidence to this.

under for the third time: he would one day come back and haunt his city, in a form and shape so water-resistant that they would never get rid of him. Not long ago, this curse manifested itself in the shape of a most extraordinary and very controversial sculpture, which – the sculptor alleges – is of Olav Kyrre.

The peaceful Olav Kyrre sitting wet, cold, and weary in his royal residence just outside Bergen, shortly before his death, grieving that the Vikings in Bergen are nice and dry, even after weeks of nothing but rain.

G: MAGNUS BARFOT (MAGNUS BAREFOOT)

agnus was a rather peculiar character in our series of royals, for which reason he is included here. He got his nickname because he enjoyed going barefoot. Whether this applied to one foot only, or to both, few or none can answer, but the question is only logical since it would have been more sensible to call him 'Magnus Barefeet' i.e. plural. 'Barfot', i.e. singular, does indicate that either he had only one foot – or he had a sock and shoe on one, and nothing on the other. Whatever: peculiar, as we have already stated.

It has been suggested by some that the reason why Magnus walked about with at least one foot bare, was a strong desire to toughen himself up, and that the term 'Having Viking blood in your veins' originated with Magnus. This blood was normally heavily diluted with mead since this had a most appealing anti-freezing effect.

In any case, Magnus died young. But not before he managed to father three boys, namely:

H: Sigurd,

I: Øystein, and

J: Olav.

The saga says that all three of them inherited their father's peculiar habit, all three being born with bare feet.

Olav died very early, thus promptly dropping out of the history. Since Magnus was their father, Sigurd and Øystein were given the surname Magnusson, and together they ruled the country wisely and well for many years under the name of MAGNUSSON BROS.

Sigurd loved travelling, and did so a lot of the time (visiting, inter alia, Israel), whilst his brother stayed at home, taking care of domestic affairs. If Sigurd liked travelling abroad,

Øystein's great hobby was hiking – walking and climbing as many Norwegian mountains as he possibly had time and energy for, in between all the wise ruling Sigurd left him to do. And it was after he had lost his way completely several times, ending up in places he had no intention of ever ending up in, (some of them he never even knew existed), that he came up with two excellent ideas which we – as well as the many tourists coming to Norway to go walking in our mountains – must be eternally grateful to Øystein for.

Øystein's first good idea, as he saw it, and rightly so, was that if – IF – you should be unlucky enough to lose your way, wandering about without the remotest idea where you were, where you were going or even who you were, your hope of ever seeing your loved ones again draining away like water in the desert, then you should at least be able to have somewhere to seek shelter for the night, or week, whatever. A roof above your head, in other words. So you could recover your senses and stake out the safest way to the nearest, inhabited valley.

By so deciding, Øystein – but probably without knowing it there and then – laid the very basis for the Norwegian Mountain Hut and Rambling Association.

His second good idea grew from the first one – it was undoubtedly the word 'stake' which triggered it, but this does in no way detract from the fact that it was an excellent idea in its own right. If, thought Øystein, all the footpaths and bridleways were *clearly marked* by means of cairns and stakes and poles and stones or whatever might be handy, there would probably be little call for the huts anyway, since you then would have to be pretty stupid to lose your way. Being a man of action, he implemented the second plan immediately, deeming it to be the more urgent of the two. The result was that when his brother returned from one of his visits abroad, and wanted to spend the first Sunday at home walking in the mountains, he could hardly take three steps without bumping into a cairn, a stake, a pole, a stone or whatever. Øystein's plan had been so thoroughly implemented that it was now difficult to walk in a straight line on *any* Norwegian mountain – the only way the ramblers could avoid constant collisions with these markers, was to snake and wind their way round, between, and inside them all.

This was later on taken up by skiers, and given the name slalåm – or 'slalom' in English.*

---

*For many years it was firmly believed that the word 'slalåm' comes from the Norwegian County of Telemark, being the two words 'sla' – meaning an even slope - and 'låm', meaning piste – where you ski. Not at all. The origin is far older than anyone has so far imagined. As we know (at least all those who have read so far), King Sigurd was a keen traveller, visiting – as mentioned already – Israel amongst other countries in that region. There, he learned the local greeting: 'Shalom'. Back home in Norway, he, like all his subjects and anyone else happening to walk about in the mountains, had to weave and snake his way in between all these rather strange obstacles his brother had put up whilst he – Sigurd – had been away. Every time King Sigurd bumped into people, weaving and snaking their way in his opposite direction, he smiled and greeted them with 'Shalom!'. Then, when winter came and the skis came down from all the attics and onto people's feet, they started skiing in between all these various objects sticking up from the snow, and someone asked one day what to call this new sport, since it really ought to have a name. The answer was that 'The King calls it 'Shalom'', which was unanimously adopted, and over the years became the more Norwegian 'slalåm'.

But it would still take a long time before this type of skiing became what it is today. It did not really become a national sport until every third Norwegian was born, not only with a pair of skis on their feet, but also with bindings. So after The Magnusson Bros patented Øystein's invention, the sport of slalåm developed gradually and steadily to our modern version.

The Magnusson Bros are most definitely and decisively the End of the Viking period – this heroic, proud part of our history.

But before leaving this period altogether, we'll give a very brief summary from Harald Hårfagre and up. It will help you to get a clearer overview of it all:

King Sigurd during one of his many and regular mountain walks towards the end of the Viking period. Note the Viking, bottom right on this picture: in spite of reasonable summer weather he has skis on his feet, probably because he is behind with regard to the previous winter – or ahead of the next one. Whatever, it must have been difficult.

SUMMARY

E MAY SAFELY SAY THAT HARALD HÅRDRÅDE WAS THE VERY LAST VIKING KING, albeit not the last Viking. It is quite correct that we have mentioned kings who came after him, all under the somewhat flexible heading 'THE VIKING PERIOD', in spite of the fact that every one of these lacked the Big Buzz of earlier kings. They all seemed to have run out of steam.

So for the sake of clarity and good order, it should be repeated that the actual and genuine Viking Period expired with King Harald Hårdråde at Stamford Bidge in the year 1066. He sets a definite and absolute full stop for the Viking Period.

The Monarchs following King Harald Hårdråde lacked The Big Buzz. They became smaller and smaller – King Inge (1135-1161) for example, measured a mere 38cms above the ground in his stocking feet, a fact which can be easily established:

We know by statistical data that the youngsters called in to do National Service – and thus the population as a whole – become taller and taller for each generation. So, by extrapolating BACK in time, since it is only reasonable to assume that we have not started growing taller all by a sudden, but that it is part of the process and progress of the entire human race, we find that the average Viking at the time of King Inge measured about 18.6cms.

*But we also know that the King was always a head taller than the average man, so 38cms would seem just about the most likely. This will also partly explain why all the Viking ships we have found have been lying so low in the ground. It is not difficult to see that for these small, but tough and rough, men to be able to board their vessels to set sail and do raids in foreign parts, the ships **had** to be low.*

Few, if any, of the following kings, carried out any deeds worth mentioning. The one and only exception might just about be King Sverre Sigurdsson. He became king in 1177 in the normal way, by beating the incumbent in a battle in the Sognefjord (the longest fjord in the world, as good a place to have a battle as any).

Sverre was determined to:
a) break the power of the (Catholic) Church in Norway, and
b) make people drink less alcohol.

The former he managed by telling the Pope, loud and clear so the latter could hear him all the way down to Rome, what he could do with his Church (Sverre even suggested the best, if not, perhaps, the most convenient way, of doing it), and the second he did by creating total confusion amongst his subjects: Sverre travelled all over and round Norway, visiting as many places as he possibly could, talking about the evils and temptations of alcohol. One result was that the relatively few who had never thought seriously about drinking alcohol, began to think that if it was really that tempting, perhaps they ought to try it . . . ?

By doing this, i.e. a) and b), King Sverre laid TWO cornerstones for future events in our country's history. Firstly, he paved the way for Martin Luther some 400 years or so later, and

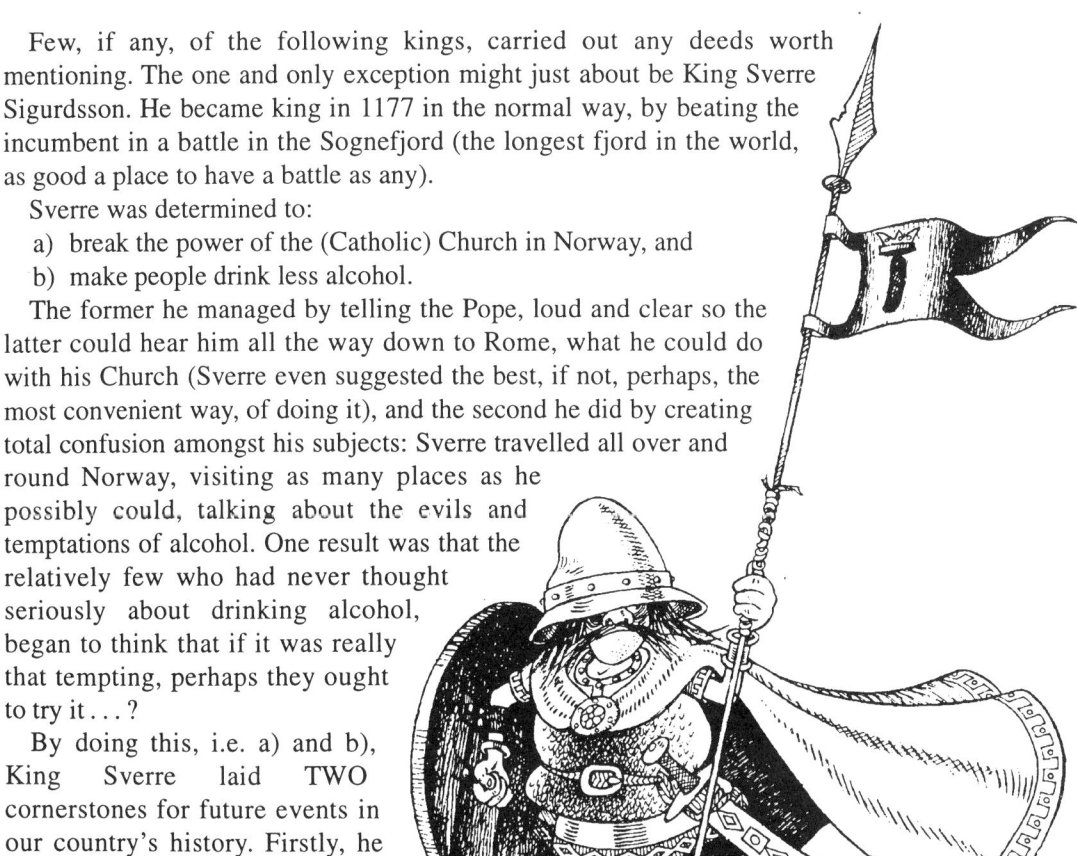

King Inge, for example, was 38cms tall. And he was no dwarf, measured by the standards of the day!

thus the Lutheran Church, and, secondly, he put the idea of a State Monopoly for Wine and Spirits into the head of later politicians and those sorts of people. There are many who think King Sverre was little short of a disaster.

Whatever: the Viking Period was most definitely over, finished, and out. But before closing the door, let us pause for a moment with Norway at the very peak of the country's power and influence, and see what might so easily have been.

We remember from the story of Harald Hårfagre that a great many of the country's best and foremost women and men, being highly critical of the way in which HH ruled the country with an iron fist, packed their bags, filled their boats, and set sail for greater promises elsewhere. It must be remembered that universal suffrage was totally unknown in those days, not only in Norway, but also in most other countries, making it difficult to change things. Not only that, even if a universal suffrage HAD existed, it would not have helped these good men and women all that much since the king could not be voted out of office (that's one of the advantages of being a king, and not a mere president). And very, very few had the will or guts to challenge Harald Hårfagre to another battle or two – had he not beaten 31 – thirty-one! - local kings and earls and all their followers in that fjord with the unpronounceable name not long ago? The one and only solution was to emigrate – and leave HH to his antics. So, as we have seen, they sailed west, to Iceland, where they went ashore, unloaded all their stuff, unpacked and – presumably – built houses. And just as well.

But before long, it got quite crowded on Iceland, as more and more unhappy Norwegians arrived, every one alleging persecution and dire troubles at home. And since a fair slice of Iceland is covered by glaciers, refusing to withdraw much even in the summer, and a lot of the rest is equally covered in sheep, there is only so much land upon which people can live. In the end, the late-comers simply had to push on in search of available land, and they discovered Greenland.

Being the largest island on this earth, it may seem more than strange (come to think of, it *is* more than strange) that Greenland had not been discovered before. How is it possible for such a huge island to just lie there without anyone knowing about it? It is far from easy to give an adequate answer; let it suffice to say that it took a Norwegian to discover it.

So: the Norwegians had now settled, and therefore ruled, both Iceland and Greenland; both islands of immense importance, and becoming even more important with a view to later developments.

We all know that the Vikings were superb navigators, and that their ships were even more superb and well ahead of their times – often also well ahead of schedule (favourable wind, following currents, etc.). THESE were the very people who laid the keel for the Norwegian Merchant Navy; the largest in the world if we reckon in tonnage per inhabitant – *even larger* if we don't count women and children.

For hundreds of years the Norwegians sailed and partly ruled the Seven Seas, and names like *Ormen Lange*, *Leif Eiriksson* and many more are held in great esteem and are honoured and praised all over the world to this day. At least by Norwegians.

> *The secret behind the Viking's amazing navigational skills was something as prosaic as the body-louse. This tiny little creature piloted them safely out onto and across the Seven Seas – and home again. When lice were shaken free from hair and beard – and remember that if the Vikings had plenty of anything, it was hair and beard – the louse ALWAYS walked towards south; towards sunshine and warmth, irrespective where it was when shaken loose. In the same way as ants' nests always face south. For obvious reasons there was quite a distance between ants' nests out on the open ocean, but the Vikings soon discovered that a handful of lice served exactly the same purpose. The loose lice were placed in an empty mead-bowl; the navigator kept an eye on them to see in which direction they started to move – and he had south.*
>
> *This primitive, but exceedingly efficient, compass, could also be used in the event of being shipwrecked. By having a suitably large and empty mead-bowl handy, each man got his own life-raft, and with guaranteed and ready access to plenty of lice, it was a relatively simple matter to navigate towards land and rescue.*
>
> *There are both historic and non-historic examples of entire crews drifting singly about in empty 10-litre mead-bowls for weeks, ALL THE TIME fully aware of exactly where South was!*
>
> *How to use a Viking compass:*

1. The mead-bowl is emptied.

2. The lice are shaken into the bowl. The more lice, the more definite the course.

3. It is now a simple matter to plot the course.

With both Iceland and Greenland settled, it was only natural that the trade and thus the maritime traffic between these two islands increased tremendously with ships shuttling to and fro.

Leif Eiriksson was one of the more regular Master Mariners sailing between these two islands, and the Saga tells us that he one day decided to find out what was further afield, hoisted the sail and let go. And that's how he and his crew discovered America.

There are those who sneer and say that the only reason WHY Leif discovered this so far undiscovered continent, was that he misnavigated like no one has ever misnavigated before or since: someone sailing from Iceland, setting the course for Greenland – the world's largest island, remember – missing it by more miles than you care to count, sailing happily by in utter ignorance without seeing anything Green or Land, can hardly be on the shortlist for the title 'Navigator of the Century'.

There are – believe it or not! – even those who question whether Leif *did* discover America at all, mistake or no mistake, but left it all to an Italian some hundreds of years later!

Let's look at the facts (and there are quite a few): even if, as some say, Leif *did* misnavigate (and who hasn't made a little mistake now and then?), there is every reason to believe that he did discover America. Indeed, it would have been virtually *impossible* for him NOT to do so. There is a law of nature, more explicitly called the Geographical Law, which quite simply states that anyone sailing west from Norway or Iceland, and steering clear of Greenland, will hit some part of the American continent sooner or later, like it or not. Even someone with a First Class Degree (Honours) in Total Misnavigation will find it beyond his capacity NOT to end up somewhere between Newfoundland and Tierra del Fuego. And even taking into consideration the Scandinavian's inbred, inborn and very strong inclination to veer off in a southerly direction, towards the sun, meaning that if you sail west, you tend to veer to port, and the corollary: if you sail east, you tend to veer to starboard, there is no way you can avoid America. It's as simple as that.

But was it misnavigation? The Saga would indicate it was not, saying Leif had a strong inkling that there was 'something out there' waiting to be discovered, reasoning that 'there must be more to life than shuttling between these two islands, trying to avoid damned ice-floes all the time.' So he decided to have go.

It is all very well for people to sail single-handed across the Atlantic today. Satellites, radio and numerous other means of communication, and assistance readily available if needed, has turned this once so fearsome and daring adventure into something the Vikings would have regarded as a pleasant form of relaxation. But for Leif to attempt to sail into the unknown, alone, would have been foolhardy to the extreme. And impossible: there was no way one single man could handle a Viking ship. To embark on his venture he needed a crew. But it was absolutely essential that not a single one of them had the faintest notion about the true purpose of the trip – or he would be crewless. As far as they were concerned, they were heading for Greenland once more.

It was not until the days went by and no land came into sight that they began to wonder – and THIS is where the mischievous rumours of misnavigation crept into history: in order to placate his increasingly restless crew, Leif called them all to a meeting before the mast, telling them that unfortunately, there had been a slight misnavigation due to the fact that when the body-lice were shaken into the mead-bowl as usual, no one realised there were some drops of mead left in the bowl, which the lice consumed with great delight. The result was that south, north, west, and east

The well-known and famous picture 'Leif Eiriksson discovers America'.

What the historians (and some authors) constantly ignore, is the sun-sail (or 'awning'), which the crew has hoisted – and clearly visible to the left on the picture – to protect them against the burning hot sun in the Gulf of Mexico.

Surely even a child will realise that Leif had no need for a sun-sail anywhere along the east coast of North-America.

However, shade was necessity, even for sun-worshipping Norsemen, during the last lap before going ashore in Yucatan, Mexico.

had, unfortunately, got a bit mixed up, but he promised them without fail that all would end well and that they would soon be ashore. Somewhere.

If any more proof is required that Leif Eiriksson discovered America long before Columbus had even taken up sailing, it is readily available, both in Norwegian textbooks, history books, and in many Norwegian homes in the form of a famous picture, quite clearly taken onboard at The Very Moment, and showing a man, suitably attired as it behoves a Viking, pointing rather excitedly to something (out of the picture) on the starboard bow, whilst other men come rushing – clearly equally excited – onto the deck from various directions. And the text, in clear, crisp letters under the picture says: '*Leif Eiriksson oppdager Amerika*' (Leif Eiriksson discovers America). It will indeed be difficult to produce more water-tight evidence.

So the real question is not IF, but WHERE: where did they land? Looking at a globe or a map (assuming it is big enough), Newfoundland would seem the natural place to land for a Viking sailing due west. But bearing in mind the natural drift southwards – as strongly prevalent among Scandinavians today as it was then – somewhere along the coast from, say Maine to New York, seems far more likely. We can probably dismiss any theory that they went ashore south of New York, since they would undoubtedly have spotted the enormous Statue of Liberty, visible from miles away, but of which there is no mention whatever in the Saga. So somewhere north of NY seems the best bet.

And here, the Saga gives us a pointer, telling us that they named it 'Vinland' (Wine Land) because of the grapes growing there. But it is only recently that scientists, archeologists, and others searching years back into history, trying to determine exactly *where* Leif and his men landed, discovered that they had all ignored the most obvious of facts which had been staring them and the rest of us in the face all along: Martha's Vineyard! Where else would this rather extraordinary name come from, if not from the Viking's 'Vinland'? It is so blatantly obvious that some of the learned minds are more than reluctant to consider it – let alone admit it, out of pure embarrassment, the ORIGINAL name having probably been 'Mørejarls Vinland' (Wine land (i.e. Vineyard) belonging to the Earl of Møre). But 'Mørejarl' is both incomprehensible and nearly unpronounceable to an English speaking person, so over the years and generations this gradually changed to the much more familiar and understandable 'Martha's', making far more sense to the modern population.

This is probably a suitable place to interrupt the author's somewhat special comprehension of where Leif Eiriksson landed on the American Continent.

By looking at any map you will immediately see that it you follow the 'louse heading South' which Leif did, both boat and crew, having passed the east coast of USA, the Florida Keys, the Bahamas, Pinar del Rio, Cuba, the Gulf of Mexico, and the Straits of Yucatan, will unavoidably end up in Puerto Morales on the Yucatan Peninsula, Mexico. The statues of Vikings should be sufficient evidence!

The author is of the opinion that had Leif sailed further South than the author thinks he did, he would have seen the Statute of Liberty and made a note of this in the ship's log. That is, with respect, sheer nonsense.

A close scrutiny of more than 800 log books from Norwegian vessels sailing regularly along the North American coast, equally regularly passing New York, has revealed that the Statue of Liberty is not mentioned even once! **Norwegian Master Mariners are not in the habit of making notes in their log books about statues of any kind!**

Nor did Leif Eiriksson!

PS: The author's description of the return journey of Leif and his men does, however, seem to be more or less in agreement with reality.

The final evidence, 1:
'The incident on the Beach'

The now so well-known incident on the Beach, where Leif Eiriksson and his men in the best Nordic tradition enjoys both women and drink in equal measures. Or even more of one than the other.

Not, perhaps, exactly an example to be followed, but then, after months at sea –.

In the background one can clearly see a local artist, ably assisted by his assistant, busy sculpting the famous statue of Leif Eiriksson, among many other Viking-inspired statues in 'The Temple of Warriors' erected in memory of the visiting warriors from far up North.

The Saga also tells us that Leif and his men went ashore in this newly discovered and unknown country. Anything else would, we must say, have been very strange indeed after so many days at sea and probably short of both food and water and whatever else.

AND JUST IN CASE THE ABOVE HAS NOT ONCE AND FOR ALL DISPELLED ANY DOUBT WHATEVER, AND THERE ARE ALWAYS SOME DOUBTERS, LET'S HEAP ON SOME MORE UNDISPUTABLE FACTS AND SOLID EVIDENCE:

It is an unknown historical fact, at least until now – that Leif and his men left their mark on the Maya culture.

But if the famous Spanish explorer Hernando De Soto (1496-1542) is to be taken seriously (and he would undoubtedly object to not to be), we have to note his important observations when he arrived at Yucatan in 1528.

According to his contemporary Spanish explorer and friend, Fransisco Pizarro (the inventor of the pizza), who founded Lima in 1534, two things startled De Soto when he came to Yucatan for the first time.

The first was that the Mayas already then realised that they were Maya-indians. The explanation is simple:

Leif Eiriksson went ashore in Puerto Morales on Tuesday, 3rd May, 1001. Thus the name.

The other was the Indians' enormous stone sculptures, showing Leif's crew in partly unrecognisable, unfamiliar, and very un-warlike positions. The local brew Black Death Tequila – drunk neat at the time – is probably to blame.

It is easy to understand that De Soto and Pizarro, as good Spaniards, wanted to keep the sensational discovery that the Vikings had already been and gone a tightly guarded secret. Had a mere word about this leaked out, it would have been like Roald Amundsen, Scott, and the South Pole all over again!!

Unfortunately for Leif the Norwegian flag had not been invented at that time, so it was not a colourful banner, flapping happily in the wind, which greeted De Soto as he stepped ashore, but life-like Vikings, cut in stone. And easy to explain away.

The fact that Hernando already several years after his death regretted his actions and stated that the sculptures at Chichen Itza showed Vikings, and nothing but Vikings, does not help much.

Nevertheless, such words, from a man who became the Governor of both Cuba and Florida, must be taken seriously when deciding exactly where Leif Eiriksson went ashore on the American Continent.

The final evidence No.2.

A surprised Hernando De Soto (to put it mildly) discovers the statue of a very relaxed and not totally sober Leif Eiriksson outside the famous 'Temple of Warriors' (Chichen Itza) when he arrives Yucatan in the year 1528.

If we compare the statue with the picture of the incident on the Beach, we will see that scrupulous souvenir-hunters have broken off and stolen Leif's mead-swinging left arm. This must have happened between 1001 and 1528!

To judge from the Saga they did not stay there all that long – not so much because they did not like grapes as the fact that they did not much like or appreciate the people growing them: they had feathers in their hair and kept flinging little axes at the Vikings (mostly missing, fortunately) – even sending the odd arrow or two in their direction.

To us, living today, this can hardly be surprising. Put yourself in the moccasins of the local inhabitants round this period. They were not so much farmers as hunters. And the sudden appearance of some fur-clad creatures, undoubtedly on all fours at times due to either over-indulgence in mead or ferreting around for edible growths, would entitle them to think that this might well be a new and hitherto unknown and therefore untested source of food – perhaps a cross between a buffalo and and a bear. Add helmets with horns, and you get the drift. Little wonder arrows and axes kept flying.

But the Vikings didn't see it that way. They had a distinct feeling they were not all that welcome, so Leif and his brave men climbed back onboard, weighed anchor, set sails and changed the course 180° in relation to the one they held upon arrival. It is possible Leif's men had slight misgivings about his ability to navigate them all safely back to their homeland which, all said and done, was a very long way away, but thought on balance that even he had a reasonable chance of finding the largest island in the world or at least a smaller one nearly next to it. Failing all that, they thought, Norway was a hell of a long country, stretching from wherever to a long way south, so *should* Leif happen to miss the two islands, he was bound to hit land somewhere between Kirkens and Lindesnes. And that was when Leif, sensing his crew's uneasiness, uttered the now so famous words, re-uttered and paraphrased so many times by professions ever since: 'Trust me, I am a navigator!'.

They didn't have much choice, really, so they did. And Leif was as good as his words. Or even better.

Because not only did they all return home, safe and sound apart from a few scratches here and there, – but there was no need for any of them ever to lift an oar or hoist another sail again to earn a living: for the rest of their lives they made more than enough to keep themselves and their families in what was at that time great luxury, by telling tall stories about Cowboys and Indians.

But the main reason – apart from all the little axes and arrows flying about – why no one followed where Leif had sailed first, was that *Alltinget* (the Icelandic Parliament) passed an Act which prohibited anyone from even considering sailing to Vinland. This decision was due to the perhaps not unreasonable assumption that a free import of grapes would have had catastrophic results: add wine and hard spirits to all the mead being consumed, and ...

Just the thought of it made every single M.A. (*Member of the Allting*) shudder. 'It would be like throwing a bucket of pure spirits on the fire,' as one of them expressed it during the debate, which turned out to be one of the shortest debates ever heard or had in the *Allting*. But many were those who did not like this decision. One of the *skalds* put it like this:

> Sad it is to see
> law-makers laying down a law
> stopping ships sailing freely on seven seas.
> All simple and bloody stupid the *Allting* sits.

For this lay, the *skald* received great acclaim from everyone but the members of the *Allting*, who did not like it at all. In fact, they disliked it so much that they started a hate-campaign against the *skald*, who was forced to flee the country shortly afterwards, well before he had had time to compose himself to produce an even more damning lay. The saga does not say where he went to, or what happened to him.

Looking at this glorious period of our country's history, what our ancestors achieved was nothing short of impressive. In addition to living in and ruling over Norway (which would only seem natural for a Norwegian), they also had large bits of Sweden; they ruled over the Orkneys and the Faroes, and a large area of the Hebrides. The Norwegian Vikings had conquered Iceland – probably without much opposition; they had Shetland and some fjord areas on Greenland under their control, in addition to being a constant threat and irritation to the King of Denmark and the King of Sweden. As if this was not enough, the Vikings even held a not insignificant amount of land in England (in particular in the North), – they had even sailed round the top of Scotland and down the other side to see what wonders they might find there. What they found was a lush, green, and often very wet island, sparsely populated by very friendly people, so they hauled their longboats up on land and settled down for a while, more or less laying the foundation – not to say the keel for – what is today called the Irish Republic, but which in those days was called something quite different.

This might, perhaps, be the right moment to pause a little and take a closer, albeit not TOO close a look, at what our forefathers did and what exactly happened over there, on that green island pushed a fair way into the Atlantic by the rest of Europe:

As mentioned immediately above, they apparently liked what they saw, and before long they had hauled their longboats up so many creeks and bays around the coast that they lost count. The rivers appealed greatly to the Vikings since these made it possible to row or sail a bit inland, away from the immediate coast, and one river in particular appealed so much to them that a King Torgjest or Turgeis (they weren't all that fussy with exact spelling, the Vikings weren't), settled on what he and his men deemed a Most Suitable Place by the river, after which he issued the Royal Decree stating that this was just the spot for a Capital City, and never mind the bogs and the damp. And that's how Dublin was born.

We make no apology for dwelling a little more on this event, not least because all the history books to date have totally misinterpreted and therefore misrepresented the facts surrounding the birth of Dublin and how the river got its name.

Thorough – extremely thorough – studies over the last few years, including a very long and very detailed interview with a Dublin taxi driver in the amicable atmosphere of one of Dublin's many delightful pubs, have revealed the true and correct circumstances, so why not take this opportunity to put it right, once and for all? (History teachers: pay attention!):

The Vikings rowed their way up to that spot by that river, probably driven more by curiosity than by design, in what we think was the year 840, or a few years before. The country they came to was not rolling in wealth and riches – there was, in fact, very little to pillage and plunder, but since the maidens were both pretty and friendly, what better reasons could a Viking have to haul the oars in, settle down and use this as a base for marauding trips to other parts of Europe?

And it was after one such very successful trip abroad, arriving back with their longships laden to the oar-holes with looted goodies, that word spread about their fabulous return as they rowed slowly up the river – slowly because of the heavy load they were carrying. So when they finally reached their home base, they were greeted by a great number of these pretty and friendly maidens, each one of them carrying a huge drinking vessel full of the very best local brew – the best way to greet a homecoming Viking.

But that was just the snag. As the Vikings' favourite, not to say only, drink was mead, which they drank in large quantities and at very short intervals, they were, of course, used to a drink with a rich, golden colour.

The brew so generously handed to them by lovely, female hands, did not have a rich, golden colour. It was, in fact, black as a winter night in the northest of Norway, and with what appeared to be some white foam on top. Even the most battle-hardened Viking would hesitate to down the stuff.

But not wanting to upset the waiting crowd ashore (the Vikings simply hated upsetting ANYBODY), they made a hurried excuse for not drinking it immediately, saying they had to make the ships fast before the river sent them headlong down to the open seas again, and promised to meet the maidens at 9.30pm that evening behind the nearest barn, after which all the landlubbers dispersed, happily, in different directions, leaving the Vikings to it.

So, left alone, every man Viking, holding a drinking vessel full of a black liquid in his hand, not knowing what to do with it, turned to his king, whose name by a quirk of fate happened to be Olav Kvite (Olav the White), asking what the hell to do with it. Olav the White was no doubt a man, a Viking, and a king who would not hesitate for a moment to take on a mighty and powerful enemy; who would not hesitate to take huge risks in raids and battles in the hope of winning gold, goods, and great victories. But he was also a man, a Viking, and a king who knew when he was faced with the impossible. And, in addition to all that, he was a man of few words. Therefore, all he did was to utter one, single word: 'Overboard!'

And so they did – every single man emptying the drinking vessel into the river. Now, this might not have been the cleanest of rivers even in those days. What with all the wetland and peat around, its waters were hardly crystal clear. But whatever the colour had been up to this point in history, it was as nothing compared to the colour it took on after all the Vikings had emptied their well-meant 'Welcome back' – liquid gifts into the little pool in the river where they had moored their longboats. It turned black.

From that day on the settlement was called nothing but 'Baile Atha Cliath' by those living there – meaning 'The Black Pool' – or 'Dublin', if you like.

Oh, yes, the river. We do not know for certain what it was called before this historic event, which – like so many historic events – was really based on ignorance and misunderstanding, but the studies and research already mentioned indicate strongly that as the now very black waters, with a white foam-like substance on the surface, drifted slowly past the longboats, one of the bearded warriors looked at it and said something along the lines of: 'It looks iffy to me', but through all the beard and many missing teeth, his shipmates next to him misheard and misunderstood him, thinking he referred to the name of the river, which has been Liffey ever since.

This one incident which, as already mentioned, was due to a complete misunderstanding and ignorance on the part of the Vikings, proved to be enough to make them change their minds about staying, uncertain of what might be offered next. (As far as we know the Vikings had, as yet, not experienced haggis in Scotland.) So when King Brian Boru offered them battle in 1014, they accepted, were beaten – and disappeared, never to come back again. A fact for which everyone living in the Republic of Ireland today should be truly grateful: hands up all those Irish women and men who today speak English with a soft, warm drawl, being understood by at least 300 or 400 million people, who would prefer to speak Old Norse, albeit also with a soft, warm drawl, but being understood only by 4 million or so compatriots, plus the odd – and probably utterly lost – Icelandic fisherman drifting by, looking for cod? Well, there you are then!

A slight correction of the author's otherwise brilliant and gripping description of this part of our history:

There were in reality **three** *(not* **two** *as mentioned by the author) important incidents that memorable evening which gave the city its name:*

As good Vikings and good Norwegians they had already THEN decided to be outside the EU. Or as King Olav expressed it: 'Better to be outside and take what you need inside, than the other way round!'

And now they returned, loaded to the oar-holes, after a very successful trip inside.

But sacking, pillage, rape, and hard rowing up numerous rivers on the Continent, takes its toll

Not only did they smell: they were in addition so filthy and dirty that it was extremely difficult to see who was the King and who was not.

So when they postponed meeting the local wenches until 9.30pm, it was simply to give themselves a chance to get rid of all the dirt and filth in the nearest pool (which, incidentally, also supplied the City's drinking water). THAT's when Olav said: 'Overboard!'

10 minutes later, and the City had lost its drinking water, but got its name, and the King would forever after be known as Olav Kvite (Olav the White). All historic ignorance would also indicate that it was after this evening – and not before – that the local brew turned black

And when one of the bearded warriors, to top it all was heard to mumble 'It looks iffy to me' as the now dirty water swilled past, the evening's quota of historic names had been more than spent!

As usual: it is the common man who has to carry the burdens!

Here, bewildered inhabitants can only establish that a mere two minutes of bathing Vikings has rendered the water completely useless as drinking water.

True, it gave the city its name, and the breweries an excellent starting point for their dark beers.

It can be seen that not even the presence of a Church representative is sufficient to clean the water.

Having thus set the record straight, and looking – at least mentally – at the map and where the Vikings had settled, it would be no exaggeration whatever to call the North Sea *Mare Norsum*.

It is, of course, tempting in a book like this to let the imagination take off in free flight: what would the world have looked like today if Leif and his fellow Vikings had been a bit more, and the members of the *Allting* a bit less, aggressive, and carried on sailing to *Vinland*, colonising the whole of North America, instead of leaving this to Spaniards, Frenchmen, and Englishmen? There is no reason to believe that the Vikings would have done this in a less successful way. On the contrary.

And with a well-established and developed *Vinland*, they could easily have moved gradually south – a direction of movement which is completely natural for all Norwegians, and colonised the rest of what is now the USA, exploring and settling further down that narrow strip just below – a small skip across the Panama Canal and into South-America where the impetus of the movement would have carried them all the way down to Tierra del Fuego.

It is a fascinating thought: they would have spoken an even broader north Norwegian dialect in Canada than in north Norway, and an even softer south Norwegian dialect in Rio than they do in Mandal today.

But such flight of fantasy has no place in a book like this, concentrating solely on hard and known facts as it does, so we shall not speculate any further. The best we can do here and now is to

DECLARE THAT THE VIKING PERIOD IS

MOST DEFINITELY OVER.

AND SO IS THIS BOOK.

WELL, IT SHOULD HAVE BEEN
But in sheer anticipation of the raised eyebrows and disappointment of all the readers (all belonging to Group 2, that is) of not being told at least *something* of what happened next, we shall give an extremely summarised summary of the next hundred years or so.

If this does not satisfy your thirst for Historical knowledge, not much will. That's all we can say.

SO:
It will be remembered that the Vikings named and arranged their kings in a clear, logical manner. A 'Harald', being son of 'Olav', would be Harald Olavsson, in the same sensible way as an 'Olav', son of 'Harald', would be Olav Haraldsson. It could not be simpler, more logical, and easier. But all this logic disappeared into historic darkness when the Viking Period expired and the Danes came more to the fore.

There is, in reality, not all that much separating Norwegians and Danes; both nations are, for example, united and in full agreement when it comes to opinions about the Swedes. And Finns, and Russians, for that matter. But when it comes to the naming of the kings, we are as far apart as penguins and polar bears. Whilst WE – the Norwegians – had a rich source of names to take from when it came to kings (Olav, Harald, Sigurd, Øystein, Inge, and many more), the Danes seemed to run completely out of imagination, settling for *only two names*: **Christian** and **Frederik**. And how!

It all started in 1448, when Christian I came onto the throne, and carried on right up to 1972 (that is *over 500 years!*) when Frederik IX died. In between these two they had no less than 9 – NINE – Christians and 8 – EIGHT – Frederiks (NINE including No. IX!).

Now, imagine you are Danish, and of school age. You have done your homework, like you should do, and your conscience is as clear as any conscience can be. Add the fact that you are a bit more interested in history than most. Or said differently: your basis for answering correctly any question posed by your teacher of history regarding virtually any aspect of Denmark's history is better and sounder than the average. Even then... Your teacher has just asked you to name the Danish king who did something terrific or specific on a certain date, and your brain is likely to flash up, instantly and immediately, something like 'Christian III', equally instantly and immediately followed by another flash saying 'Frederik II' – and yet another saying 'Christian IV' – and 'Frederik III'. In short, with a mere TWO names to play round with over a period spanning more than 500 – FIVE HUNDRED! – years, how on earth do you sort one from the other?

It causes complications – immense complications – not only for the average Dane and everyone else, but also for members of the Danish Royal Family (a simple question like 'And how is Christian today?' will in all likelihood get the reply: 'Which Christian do you mean?').

It was in a desperate attempt to try and keep some sort of order and sequence in it all that the Danes thought up the idea of *numbering their kings*, like horses in a horse race! That is all very well once you get into slightly higher numbers, but anyone seeing, say, 'Christian I' for the first time, will invariably ask themselves: 'Christian I. WHAT?', naturally thinking the roman figure 'I' (and they always use ROMAN figures for some odd reason) is a capital 'i', and therefore indicating a middle name, as in 'Harry S. Truman', and therefore that the fellow's surname is missing.

It is not until you get a bit further out in the lineage that you realise your mistake. BUT – and this is just as important a point – BUT having done that, you are not much further! Discussing Denmark's history with a Dane – ANY Dane – is a flummoxing exercise at the best of times. It is, in short, something which should be avoided at all costs, and which no doubt explains why Denmark changed to a Queen in 1972.

The reason for bringing all these Christians and Frederiks into all this (and there are an awful lot of them as you will have gathered) is that Norway and Denmark ended up as one country, or, at least, a 'United Kingdom', not long after the expiry of the V.P.

The incident which led to this union, was, quite briefly, as follows:

There happened to live in Denmark a king by the name of Valdemar (now, there's a Danish king without a number attached!). Because he was so incredibly fond of sleeping, and extremely reluctant to get up in the morning, asking his swains as he slowly opened his eyes, peering against the daylight:

Nej, er det nu atter en dag!' (lit: 'Oh, no – not ANOTHER day!'), he very soon got the nickname 'Atterdag', i.e. King Valdemar Atterdag (King Valdemar Another day).

It is hardly surprising that this Valdemar had a daughter, Margrete. She fell hook, line, and sinker for a handsome Norwegian king, Håkon Magnusson (also called Håkon VI, the Danish way), and married him. They had a son whom they called Olav, and he became King of Denmark after his grandfather, the very same Valdemar, who dropped off for good one evening at the table. King Håkon VI died in 1380, which meant Olav, King of Denmark, inherited Norway. This inheritance was not spent until 1814, when Norway decided that it was far too confusing and complicated with all these Frederiks and Christians, and declared Unilateral Independence – and joined Sweden instead. But that's a totally different story.

The opinions are still very divided as to whether Norway had any benefit whatever from the union with Denmark. But they shouldn't be. Had it not been for that union, we would have no 17th May (the day our Independence from Denmark was signed in 1814) – a date as important and celebrated as noisily in Norway as 14th July in France and/or 4th July in the US of A.

And just think of the chaos if Norway – probably as the only country in the world – had a calendar *with no 17th May*!

And not only that: with their famous Tivoli Gardens in Copenhagen, charming little villages along the coast, and their rather appealing wine-prices, Denmark is welcome to inherit us again.

It would serve them right!

King Valdemar wakes up in the middle of the night, lifts the sheepskin-blanket and asks his valet if it is another day. His valet must regrettably inform him that it is not, and asks the King to repeat the question closer to dawn. The King did so, causing him to be given the now so famous nickname.

Many have asked exactly WHEN King Valdemar asked his now so famous question. Was it early morning? During the day? In the evening – or even at night?

The answer is yes and no. As is apparent from the picture, the King first woke up sometime during the night, and was politely, but firmly, asked by his valet to go back to sleep, only to wake again when the cock crowed, i.e. at the correct time.

THERE IS NO POINT IN LOOKING

ANY FURTHER:

THERE ARE NO MORE PAGES!